Surprisingly

Playing for Hearts, Book 5

Debra Kayn

Author of *Secretly* and *Conveniently*

F+W Media, Inc.

Published by
Crimson Romance
an imprint of F+W Media, Inc.
10151 Carver Road, Suite 200
Blue Ash, OH 45242. U.S.A.
www.crimsonromance.com

ISBN 10: 1-4405-6655-0
ISBN 13: 978-1-4405-6655-4
eISBN 10: 1-4405-6656-9
eISBN 13: 978-1-4405-6656-1

Cover art © 123RF/Andrey Tsidvintsev

Chapter One

Crista Johnson gritted her teeth and tried to concentrate on what Janelle, her next door neighbor, had been droning on about for the last fifteen minutes. Paisleys were coming back? Summer colors were darker and brighter? Janelle's endless talk about her modeling career and fashion statements bored her. Crista only required breathable material that hugged her body and moved with her. She wasn't dressing to please others; she had to compete with other athletes.

She still hadn't figured out what her neighbor saw in her and kept her coming over all the time. Crista wore yoga pants or bicycle shorts most days, and her swimwear consisted of a crossback one piece designed for speed and comfort. Obviously, none of that mattered to the high fashion-conscious Janelle.

"What do you think?" Janelle set down her ice water on the patio table between them and instantly studied her pink manicured false fingernails.

Crista looked down at her own blunt cut bare nails. She had no idea what the woman was going on about because all she could think of were a million ways to get Janelle to go back to her apartment. "I'm not sure."

"Exactly. I told Devon, my manager, it was impossible to lose two pounds by Friday. Not even if I took the pills to speed up my metabolism. I'll have to wear the wrap during the whole group bikini shot … like you would if you had to wear a swimsuit in public." Janelle leaned her six-foot tall body back in the chair and crossed her long, slender legs. "I'll be blacklisted from ever working with this magazine ad again, and the other girls will talk in the dressing room about the lard ass … me."

Crista glared. One more insult and she'd slap the bitch. That would end Janelle's habit of always invading her apartment.

The doorbell rang. Crista jumped out of her chair, relieved to have an excuse to walk away. "Excuse me. That's my friend Bruce. He's in town, and I promised him he could stay with me."

"Mm … details, girlfriend." Janelle sat up straighter.

Crista paused. "What are you talking about?"

"You know—his occupation, his rating, and his reputation with women. I want to know everything." Janelle fluffed her hair and shifted her breasts in her bra. "Don't leave anything out."

Crista stood at the sliding door wanting to escape, but she knew Janelle well enough to know she wasn't going anywhere until Crista provided all the juicy details. The supermodel hunted men for sport.

"I guess he's around six feet four inches tall, rugged, um, blond—" The doorbell rang again, and she cleared her throat. "Two hundred and twenty pounds maybe, I'm not sure."

Janelle sighed and waved her hand in front of her. "Never mind. You lost me at rugged."

"I'll be right back." Crista disappeared inside the house and skipped to the door, glad to avoid telling Janelle her best friend was a world-class bass fisherman. For some reason that attracted all the women, and she'd never get Janelle to go home.

She hadn't seen Bruce for four months, since they'd gone to watch their mutual friend, Juan Santiago, win his third gold in the Winter Olympics for downhill skiing. Afterward, Bruce had flown to Venezuela for a fishing tournament, and she'd come back home to California to train for the Ironman in October.

She opened the door, smiling. "You're here."

"Hey." Bruce scooped her drink out of her hand and took a sip. "That's what I call service, sweetheart."

She fisted her hands on her hips. "Greedy."

"I'll share." He handed it back after draining half the glass. "Are you sure it's okay if I crash here?"

"You don't even have to ask. You're my best friend. *Mi casa* and all that." She motioned him inside and shut the door behind him. "I even made us reservations for tonight. Does seafood sound good?"

"Down at that little restaurant on Fisher's Bay?" He threw his bag beside the couch.

"Yep, that's the place. I remembered you enjoyed it last time you were in town," she said. "They have the best shrimp out of all the restaurants in town."

The sliding door opened. She caught Bruce straighten and take in her neighbor. Men. They were all the same. See a supermodel, and everything and everybody else ceased to exist.

"Janelle, this is my friend Bruce Coldwell." She turned to Bruce. "My neighbor, Janelle Langdon."

Bruce glided in front of her, and lifted Janelle's hand. "It's a real pleasure to meet you."

Crista watched the exchange and wrinkled her nose over Bruce patting his stomach as if Janelle would faint at the sight of his six pack.

"Uh huh." Janelle dismissed him and looked at Crista. "I'm leaving. You'll come Friday, right?"

Friday? Friday? What did Janelle say she wanted me to do?

She shrugged. "I don't know … "

"Please come." Janelle towered over her, bouncing on her toes. "Everyone who is anyone will be there. It's the function of the season, and it's not all supermodels. The press and photographers will be there too, and the timing is perfect for you. You want opportunities for that … race thing you do, so you have to come."

The motion of Janelle's boobs dancing in the halter top made Crista motion sick. She grabbed her friend's arms, stopping her from moving. "Yes, I'll be there. I'll call you Friday to get more information." Janelle clasped her hands to her perfect chest. "Goody. Except, I'll call you. I'm supposed to have my nails redone that day, and I don't want to answer the cell if I'm sitting in the chair at the salon. Then later, I'll help you pick out something sexy to wear."

"That's okay. I'm sure I can figure out something to wear on my own." She glanced at Bruce and found him grinning.

Kill her now. Bruce would never let her hear the end of her girly adventure. She'd rather gain attention for being a trainer, an athlete, competing in long distance running or swimming, not for showing up to flaunt her body and get her picture taken on the off chance she hit the middle pages of a magazine somewhere.

"No way." Janelle air kissed her cheeks. "Friends help each other, and I want you to look beautiful. We need to get rid of the athletic look and start making you look like a real woman. A single, feminine woman who is open and available to men."

"I'm not in the dating market," Crista said.

Janelle waved her hand, dismissing Crista's statement. "That's why you need to have a fling. There will be plenty of married men at the party, alone and desperate, and looking for someone like you."

"Absolutely not." Crista clenched her teeth. Janelle's habit of only going after men who were taken disgusted her. "I think it's time for you to go, so I can catch up with my *friend*."

Janelle bounced past without saying goodbye to either her or Bruce. When the door shut, Crista flopped down in the chair and groaned. She needed to nip her friendship with Janelle to casual status before she ended up saying something rude and causing a catfight.

Bruce sat down on the couch. "Who was that gorgeous friend of yours?"

"My bubble-headed next door neighbor slash supermodel slash pain in the ass," she muttered. "I can't stand her, so if you have an idea on how I can distance myself from someone who likes to Velcro themselves to my back, let me know."

"Set us up." Bruce inhaled deeply. "I want to get to know her better."

"You're kidding. Dating her would be suicide." She stuck her lower lip out and blew a stray strand of hair out of her eyes. "She eats men like you for breakfast and then runs into the bathroom to make herself throw up so she doesn't gain weight. It wouldn't be pretty."

"Who cares?" He propped his feet on the coffee table. "I'm not planning on a long term relationship. It's all about the sex for me nowadays."

"Ugh." Crista held up her arms and waved her hands side to side. "Spare me the details. What you do on your own time is your business."

"So, you'll set us up?"

She sighed heavily on a groan. "Honestly, Bruce. She's … complicated. Since I've known her, she has a thing for men who are already attached to other women. She enjoys the chase. Married, engaged, serious relationship, it doesn't matter. She wants to one-up any woman and prove she's all that with a topping of sprinkles."

"Have you seen her?" Bruce chuckled. "She's fucking gorgeous. Her body is killer. I can ignore what comes out of her mouth or how she acts around other women by keeping her mouth busy. She can't talk if she's giving me a bl—"

"You won't even catch her attention." She shook her head. "I'll tell you in your language, so you can understand what I'm saying. The bitch is a piranha. She'll only go for you if you're attached to a girlfriend."

"I fish for a living." He grinned, giving her a creepy I-know-something-you-don't-know look. "I know my bait."

She glared. "What are you talking about?"

"You and me. If she thinks I'm your boyfriend who showed up in town and will be staying with you, she'll be easier to hook and tag," he said, puffing out his chest. "It'll be another trophy catch I can sit back and brag about to the guys in my old age. Once I pull her in, appreciate the catch, I'll let her go back in the water for the other men in the world to enjoy."

"Speak in layman terms." Crista blinked at him, lost in Brucespeak.

"The more she watches me getting friendly with you, the more tempted she'll be to steal me away." He twined his fingers together and clasped them behind his head. "I don't spend all my time on the water. I know women. Some females would even call me an expert. Other men only wish they knew what I know."

She snorted. "I'm trying to de-friend myself from her. With my luck, you two would fall madly in love, and I'd be stuck with you both for a lifetime. You, I can handle. Her … hell no. She's a deal breaker in our relationship."

"I'll take her off your hands." He raised his brows. "Then you won't have to break her heart when you lock the door on her. I'll be getting busy in her apartment. Besides, I have two weeks here. If I get together with her, I won't have to sleep on your couch the whole time."

"I'll think about it," she said, lying to him. If she thought anymore about Janelle and Bruce getting together, she'd have her own puking problem.

Just imagining what could happen if those two hooked up made her sick to her stomach. She did not want to hear about Bruce's sex life, at all. Out of her and Bruce's mutual friends, he was the one man who'd never tried to date her. He never even flirted when he drank too much. Nothing was going to come between them. He was her best friend.

"Oh, hey." He leaned over and pulled his duffle bag closer. "I got you something in Venezuela."

She leaned forward, trying to peer inside his bag. "What?"

"This." He passed her a sack. "Open it."

She grinned, glancing at him when she opened the bag. "You really should've."

"I knew you'd bug me if I didn't bring you something back. I forget one time to buy you a surprise while I'm traveling, and I hear about it every time I call you."

She pulled out a small wicker basket, the size of an ice cream dish. Inside the rim, paintings of purple and white orchids lined the bowl. She studied it closer, and noticed the inside of the flowers had red painted dots.

"It's beautiful." She smiled, warmed from the gift. "Thank you. I think I'll put it on my dresser and use it to hold my earrings."

"Uh." He stifled his laughter. "Good idea."

"What's so funny?" she asked.

"The Venezuelan women set it on their nightstand. It's a—" he barked out a laugh, "good luck totem for fertility."

His snorts and chuckles filled her small apartment. She rolled her eyes. Honestly, why were they still friends?

Each time he visited, she looked forward to the surprise gift he brought her, a sign that he appreciated their friendship as much as she did. And every single time, he turned into a twelve-year-old boy who'd rather snap her bra than show his true feelings regarding their friendship by buying her a T-shirt or souvenir like she always begged him to.

"I'll put it in the bathroom next to the phallus-shaped coconut you brought me back from the Bahamas last year." She rolled her eyes, because once he started to outdo her in the gift giving department, he went all out to give her the funniest, most useless gift

She walked out of the room and continued the conversation. "Talk about an item that causes a lot of questions from friends. The coconut gets more attention than I do. I'm going to get you next time. That's two gifts in a row you've blown. I'm upping the competition the next time I travel. You'll get the ugliest and most useless gift I can find. You're going down."

This meant war. He'd burned her so many times with his choice of gifts, she'd lost count. She'd have to step up her game. The backscratcher she brought home from Hawaii for him to use when he was alone and had no one to scratch his itch didn't compare to an edible penis or fertility bowl.

"So, are you going to be my girlfriend?" Bruce called from the other room.

She walked back. "Whatever. If it'll get you out of my hair for two weeks after putting up with *that* gift, I'm willing to do anything."

"Great." He snatched her cell phone off the table and tossed it to her. "You and Janelle have plans to go out on Friday. All you have to do is call and tell her you want to bring your … lover. Use that exact word, too. Lover."

The way he over exaggerated the pronunciation would've made anyone laugh. She snorted, shaking her head to keep from falling into his trap. During his absence, Bruce had sunk to a new level. He must be desperate.

"You're sick. You know that, don't you?" She dialed Janelle's number, curling her lip. "I'm sure she's going to know I'm lying through my teeth."

Her soon-to-be *unfriend* picked up on the second ring. "Hello?"

"It's me … Crista." She turned around because Bruce was staring at her. "I'm calling about the party on Friday. I wasn't thinking when you were here, but I can't leave Bruce alone when he's expecting to spend every spare moment with me. So, I was wondering if I could bring my, um, *lover* to the party, too?"

"You have a lover?"

Janelle didn't have to sound shocked. Crista's shoulders sagged. She had three men she'd slept with in the past. Not boyfriends, more like one night stands with men she knew having sex with would be safe. God, she wasn't a prude.

She cleared her throat. "Yes. You met him. Bruce."

"Oh," Janelle said. Crista wasn't sure, but she thought she heard a higher lift in her voice.

She waited. In the phone, she could hear Janelle tapping her ninja-sized nails. "What do you think? Will it be okay?"

"I guess."

"Fabulous." She pretended to sound excited. "I'll see you Friday. Bye."

She disconnected the call and pretended to gag. No way was this going to work. Janelle wasn't stupid.

Bruce held his palms up. "Well? Do we have a date?"

"Yeah." She glared in his direction. "We've got a date for Friday night."

"I told you she'd go for it. Can I predict women or what?" Bruce stretched back out and crossed his ankles. "And because you did this favor for me, I'll pay for dinner tonight."

Bruce seemed really excited about the Janelle prospect. She tilted back her head and closed her eyes, praying for intervention. The last thing she wanted to do was go to the party. Not even pretending to date her best friend would provide enough entertainment to make up for being stuck making nice to a room full of models.

Chapter Two

Bruce and Crista sat alone on the patio at Fisherman's Bay overlooking the Pacific Ocean. Bruce appreciated Crista putting some thought into their first night together. The seventy-degree weather, the breeze coming off the ocean, and comfortable companionship relaxed him more than anything did after a busy trip.

Well, except for sex, and Crista in her own way was going to help him out there, too.

If he got lucky, he'd soon have a rousing tumble between the sheets with a knockout supermodel. He glanced at the water. Then he'd go to Moses Lake and win the next bass tournament.

"I'm stuffed." Crista wiped her fingers off on her napkin. "I can't believe I ate so much."

He pushed his empty plate out of the way and leaned his elbows on the table. He watched, fascinated, at the way her not-quite-shoulder-length hair kept blowing a wayward strand in her mouth whenever she tried to talk or take a bite of food.

"What's your schedule like these days?" he asked.

"I do an hour run in the morning, followed by an hour on the bike, and two hours of laps in the swimming pool in the evening. Seven days a week." She sipped her beer. "Besides doing clinics and speeches when I can find any extra time, I teach a two-hour training class twice a week in the gym at the apartment. I have a contract with the manager of the building to work off rent by giving classes, which is nice and freeing. He also gives me time off to do the Ironman in exchange for free advertising for the classes."

"Four months until the big race." He whistled. "Are you still thinking about making this your last Ironman event?"

"It depends. My goal was to go out on a win—which I think I'm capable of doing again, but the right job hasn't landed in my lap." She shrugged, hooking the pink striped strand of hair that ran along the curve of her cheekbone behind her ear. "I'm probably in the best shape of my life, but you know my desire to be in the best shape possible and the enjoyment I get from competition always leaned more toward training others. I went to Kona last December to help in a three-week training program for the sole purpose of proving to myself that I'm up for another year of competition. God, you should've seen the trouble I had. The high winds on Kawaihai Harbor almost knocked me off my bike. It's just time to retire from competition while I still have the energy."

"One of your problems is you're too small." He lifted his mug and eyed her over the rim. "Now if you were Janelle's size … you'd have no problems staying on your bike."

She curled her lip. "She's six inches taller, but I bet I'm at least twenty pounds heavier. So, your theory sucks. She'd tip over if I blew on her."

"Mm hm." He winked in male appreciation for knockout supermodels, and she threw her wadded napkin at him. "Blow her …"

"At least I'm maturing faster than your one track mind. It's time for me to go in a new direction." She sighed, her blue eyes narrowing on him. "What about you? Where are you off to next?"

"After I'm done visiting you, I'm entered into the Pacific Northwest Moses Lake Tournament to defend my reigning championship for the states." He scratched his whiskered jaw. "When that's over, I believe I'm teaching a fishing seminar to raise money for the Children's Hospital in Seattle. Then I might take a break until next spring. I'm getting burnt-out on traveling."

"Geez, it sounds like we're both getting too old for our sports." She laughed. "You're in your prime. Thirty-six years old and the world's at your beck and call. And, someone else pays your way. I envy you. There's no free ride in the Ironman, and the older I get, the harder it becomes to stay at the top."

He lowered his voice. "It's lonely. I thought I'd never admit that, but it's true. I need to settle down and stay in one place. At least contain my travels to one season. I have a house in Napa Valley, a new home on the coast of Oregon, and a cabin in the Gifford National Forest up in Washington state. Yet I spend more time sleeping on my friends' couches than I do enjoying what I have."

She nodded. "Before long, you'll drop out of singlehood the way the rest of our friends have in the last couple of years. First Grayson, then Dominic, even Juan, and now Gary found someone to make him happy."

"What about you? Ever think of tying the knot?"

"Yeah. I think about it. Sometimes." She looked at her watch. "We better head back. I want to get swim time in before the pool closes. Do you feel like pushing me on the laps?"

"When have I ever turned down being in the water?" He laughed at her challenge. "I'll even give you a twenty second start."

"You're so going down." She stood and looped her arm through his. "It's nice to have you here."

"Tell me that when you're dragging my sorry ass out of the pool." He strode along the dock, making her hurry to keep up with his longer legs. She'd outswim him. The least he could do was make her work to keep up with him on land.

A half hour later, dressed in swimwear with their towels hung around their necks, Bruce and Crista exited her apartment and headed for the elevator. He flicked her ass with his towel. She screamed and jumped to the other side of the hallway to avoid another sting.

"You are so paying for that." She held her stance and wound the length of her weapon in her hand. "Prepare to die."

The end of the towel snapped him on the chest. He winced and set foot after her, not willing to let her win.

She shimmied quickly and then ran. He took his time because the hallway came to a dead-end only ten feet away. He had her cornered.

He aimed and prepared to do damage. She dropped her towel and held her hands out in front of her. "Don't do it."

"Dance, sweetheart, dance." He flicked her feet. "Say it … "

"No." She hopped side to side, avoiding the stinging end of the towel. "Never."

"Faster." The white towel blurred in front of her and he laughed. Damn, she was light on her feet.

She screamed and plastered herself against an apartment door. "Okay. Okay. Bruce Coldwell, you are *the* man."

"I'll take that for now. Next time, I want you to do better. I prefer you to acknowledge my stamina and prowess." He wiggled his brows. "Feel free to compare me to the coconut in your bathroom, if you prefer."

She shook her head and laughed, trying to catch her breath. "Your ego is going to kill you one—"

One second she was pressed against the door, and the next she fell through open air. He rushed forward, but not before her ass took the brunt of the fall. Hard.

He squatted, grimacing. "Sorry, sweetheart. Are you all right?"

Crista blinked up at him, lost in the mishap and reaching for him. He stroked her cheek and kissed her forehead. "Just sit there for a second and get your breath."

Crista nodded, clutching his hand. He inhaled deeply, hoping she was okay. He felt awful. He should've seen what was happening and stopped her from falling.

"Better?" he asked.

She moistened her lips. "Yeah, I think."

"What are you doing on the floor, Crista?" Janelle stood behind Crista, looming over them both.

The legs he'd admired earlier on Crista's neighbor stretched on forever. He trailed his gaze from her high heels on up to the high hem of her dress at the top of her thighs. He blew his cheeks out, unable to stop staring. Crista slapped his arm, and he stood, helping her off the floor.

She let him pull her up, but wrinkled her nose at the movement. "It's the agony of defeat."

Bruce frowned. "Sorry. I had no idea the door would open."

"It's okay." She rubbed her backside. "My fault. I wasn't watching what I was doing."

"I'm glad you came over." Janelle grabbed Crista's arm, tugging her away from Bruce. "I want you to tell me which outfit I should wear tomorrow night."

"We weren't coming over." Crista grabbed Bruce's hand and pried herself away from Janelle. "We're on our way to the pool."

"That's not important. The pool is open around the clock." Janelle tossed her hair over her bare shoulder.

"Uh." Crista glanced at the skimpy black cocktail dress hugging Janelle's curves. "You look great."

Great? Janelle looked fantastic. Mind blowingly sexy, in Bruce's opinion.

"Not this one, silly. I need to change into them." Janelle stepped back. "Come on, I'll show you."

"We really need to go." Crista stepped over to stand beside him. "Another time, maybe?"

Janelle's lower lip came out. "Please?"

Bruce clamped his teeth to keep from grunting at the erotic scene and nudged Crista with his elbow. "Are you sure you're okay, 'cause …"

She turned her gaze to him and frowned. He widened his eyes and flicked them toward Janelle without turning his head. *Come on, read the signs.*

Crista's brows pinched together, and she tilted her head. He nodded slowly, hoping she'd understand that he'd do anything, anything within his power, to get inside that woman's apartment. He inhaled in relief when Crista's mouth formed an O in understanding.

"You know what you need? A man to give you his opinion." Crista pushed Bruce toward her. "Take my boyfriend. He's great at clothes and not that great at swimming. He'd be happy to help you while I do my laps."

"Please, tell me he doesn't help you pick out your clothes." Janelle looked down her rather perfect nose at her. "I require a man who has tastes in fashion."

"He doesn't," Crista mumbled. "But he's gone to many fashion shows, dated a gazillion models, and is a world-class bass fisherman. He knows bait."

"Bait?"

Crystal and Bruce made a good team, and it was time to step in and do his part. He cleared his throat and shrugged nonchalantly. "I know what attracts men to women."

Great. Now he sounded like Dr. Phil. He leaned against the doorframe. If he played aloof and unresponsive to her charms, she'd have no choice but to invite him to her bed.

Janelle trailed her gaze along Bruce's body, inspecting him. He lifted the corner of his mouth, letting her know he approved of her attention. She must've found him up to par because she turned her back and walked into the apartment without another word, leaving the door open.

Bruce leaned down and kissed Crista's cheek. "Thanks. I owe you, sweetheart. Don't wait up."

Then he trailed after Janelle, and the door closed extra loudly behind him. His thoughts shifted from what kind of gift he'd buy Crista for helping him bag the supermodel to what he planned to do to the supermodel in bed, or in the living room. His step had an extra jump. Hell, he'd even do her out on the terrace. He wasn't picky.

Inside Janelle's apartment, he couldn't help but compare it to Crista's pad in size, but that's where the likenesses ended. Crista had decorated hers in pastel blue and nautical objects she'd collected on the beach. His lungs constricted and he gazed around in stunned silence. Janelle had styled hers after a Marilyn Monroe movie. Black and white. Nude sculptures. Seductive photos blown into posters. He peered closer at one scantily clad picture of a woman bent over the back of a couch. *Shit.*

He knew those legs, those breasts, those hips. The woman in the picture was Janelle herself.

Janelle caught him ogling the picture. "Well?"

He turned. His chest tightened and his balls smiled.

A red shimmery dress hugged her curves. The high neck accented the holes at the sides of her ribs, showing off the indentions to her waist. "It's nice."

"Nice?" A tiny squeak came from Janelle, and she stomped back into her room.

The shiny material of the dress soaked in a little salmon egg juice would make a perfect trolling lure for trout fishing. He glanced back at the picture on the wall. Now that's a woman who'd please a man in bed. He wouldn't mind having her recreate that exact same pose for him tonight.

Her heels clicked across the wooden floor and she snapped her fingers. "Pay attention."

"I'm all eyes, baby," he mumbled, taking her all in.

She stuck her hip to the side and placed her hand on her waist. "Which one is better? The last dress or this lighter dress?"

Now she was talking his language. He slowly strolled around her, taking in the indention of her waist, the slope of her ass, the flat stomach. The sleek white material showed everything, even her braless nipples. Behind her, he bit his tongue. *Damn.*

"Well?" she said.

"Definitely this dress." He moved around her, skimming her arm, and stood in front of her. "Yeah, this one."

She narrowed her eyes. "Why?"

He trailed his finger over the thin spaghetti strap. "It shows off your shoulders."

She nodded in agreement. "I do have great arms."

"Yes." He looked lower. The deep dip in the front barely contained her breasts. "It screams sexy."

Her lips quivered in pleasure and she finally allowed herself to smile. "Yes. That's the reaction I'm going for."

He moved back and sat down on the couch, making himself at home. She continued smiling, and turned for his enjoyment. He leaned over to watch her swish her ass out of the room. *That's it, baby; go slip into something more comfortable.*

She stopped at her bedroom door, looked over her shoulder, and raised her brows in question. He stood, ready to follow her anywhere, when she fluttered her hand toward him. "You're dismissed."

He stopped in his tracks. "Excuse me?"

"You may run back to your little lover. I'm through with needing you." She pointed in the direction of the door as if he didn't understand English.

He pivoted and walked to the door. Maybe he was losing his touch. Typically, women enjoyed him. They found him attractive. He'd even had more than a few past girlfriends who'd had a hard time understanding they were through and begged him to take them back. But dismissed?

Shit.

He entered Crista's apartment, glad she wasn't back to see his humiliation, and crashed on the couch. At least nothing in her place reminded him of sex every five seconds. Though, now that he thought about it, he had seen sexy black lingerie draped over

Crista's bedroom chair when he'd asked her where he should put his luggage. He sat up, cocked his head, and thought about looking again to make sure he hadn't been hallucinating. He exhaled and lay back down. It was probably one of Crista's girlfriends'. She wouldn't wear something like that. She was more the boy shorts and sports bra kinda girl.

He rubbed his hands over his eyes. Going without sex for four months was fucking with his head. He wasn't supposed to think about what Crista wore under her clothes.

An hour later, he'd concluded that he'd have to become more aggressive if he was going to bag Janelle. Ms. Piranha needed to realize she couldn't toy with him the way she did most men. Hell, he fished for a living, fought bears coming down to the river, swam with sharks, and battled white rapids in a canoe. He even wore a flannel shirt most days. Yet she'd dismissed him as if he was her assistant. *Screw that.*

The door opened and Crista walked into the kitchen. He rolled off the couch, strolled over, and stood beside the sink, waiting for her to finish relieving her thirst.

He tapped her on the arm. "Hey."

She screamed and pressed her hand to her chest. "Shit. Don't do that. Make some noise or something to let me know you're here. You freaked me out. I thought you'd still be at Janelle's apartment."

A muscle in his jaw twitched, and he rubbed the offending spot. "We need to step up our game plan."

"Gave you the cold shoulder, huh?" She smirked in enjoyment.

"Yeah." He shrugged the disappointment off and forged ahead. "This is going to take more work than I thought. Tomorrow night. We'll show her what she's missing out on."

"How?"

"By showing her how I satisfy you sexually."

Chapter Three

The beach house where the party was located loomed above the ocean in a mix of contemporary galore and extremely high windows. Inside the foyer, Crista discreetly readjusted the top of her dress. *Oh, boy.*

The material amounted to little more than a white baby-doll nightie. She clamped her arms to her side. Bruce had surprised Crista with the dress this afternoon. She scooted further behind him in the crowded room and snuck a glance to make sure the bodice still contained her breasts. Any excess movement on her part, and she'd be flashing the crowd faster than a college student on spring break.

Bruce grabbed her hand, bringing her around and in front of him. "Stop fidgeting. You look hot."

His hands went to her hips and he pulled her back to his chest. She stiffened, afraid his touch would expose her to the crowd. "I can't believe I'm wearing this."

"It's sexy."

"Maybe on a mannequin. Did you even stop to think about what the dress would look like on me?" She peered up and over her shoulder at him. "There's not enough material to cover my boobs. I'm larger than you think I am."

His body moved in silent laughter. "Don't cut yourself short."

"I'll nail you if you compare my height to Janelle's," she said on a hiss. "This isn't going to work. Janelle's not even paying us any attention. She hasn't looked our way or even glanced at me."

"You're right about that part. Let's work our way around the room and stand beside her." He skimmed his fingers down her arm and grabbed her hand. "Strut if you can."

"Strut?"

"Yeah." He glanced down at her. "You know, wiggle your ass."

She would not. Besides, he walked too fast, and her breasts were building momentum. She'd be lucky to make it safely to their destination without doing a strip tease dance for every single person in the room.

She walked with her chin tilted to keep an eye on her wandering body parts, until she collided with a warm body. She planted her hands on a solid chest and raised her gaze. A man in a black silk shirt blocked her path. "I'm so, so sorry. I wasn't watching where I was going."

"It's not every day a gorgeous woman stumbles into my path." His smile was pleasant, but his eyes leered. "Please, tell me you're here alone."

"No. I came with … " She glanced beside her for Bruce, but he'd left her side. In the crowd walking out onto the dance floor, she couldn't spot him. "I guess I am."

"My name's Brady Charden." He lifted her hand and brought it to his lips. "It's wonderful to bump into you."

Oh. My. God. She tittered, sounding as if she'd never had a man introduce herself before. Which wasn't the case, because there were lots of men she talked to everyday. But she *knew* this guy. Well, knew his name.

He was a famous photographer. Not for models, but he captured wildlife in exotic locations and his work was plastered all over *National Geographic*.

"Crista Johnson." She carefully extracted her hand from his grasp. "It's nice to meet you, too."

He tilted his head, leaned in closer, and said, "Would you like to dance with me, seeing as you're here all alone, and I've found myself needing a dance partner?"

"I'd love to."

What was she doing? Her dress was not made for moving around on the dance floor in front of everyone. She looked around the room one more time, half hoping Bruce would save her, and yet wanting to dance with Brady.

Obviously, she'd lost her pretend date. She followed Brady out to the middle of the floor. Behind his back, she hitched up the top of her dress again and prayed the music wouldn't change. Slow was good.

Brady swept her into his arms. She put her arms around his shoulders, plastered herself against him to keep the material over her breasts in place, and let him take the lead. He knew how to dance.

Not too tall, and rather sexy in a polished, suit and tie kind of way, he smiled at her. "You're very beautiful."

She practically floated across the floor. "Thank you."

"I thought for a moment you'd come with a boyfriend, but he seems to have wandered off without you. I know if I had a girlfriend and she looked like you, I wouldn't leave her side." His hand wandered lower on her back.

She sucked in her breath, and her dress slipped further down. "Oh?"

"I don't think I've seen you at one of the sponsored functions before. Are you a model?"

"No, not at all. I'm a professional athlete ... triathlon." She ducked her chin, peeked at her cleavage, and relaxed. Still covered. "Training is a year round sport and keeps me busy."

"Really? How fascinating. You must be in great shape." His fingers dug into the curve where her back ended and her butt started.

She inched back, trying to put some space between them. "Y-yes. That's the goal."

"Darling!" Janelle materialized beside her, and before Crista could answer, she was whisked away from Brady.

Crista found herself twirled in a circle, no longer dancing, no longer beside Brady, no longer star-struck. She was pissed.

She pressed her hand to her chest and glared at Janelle. "What are you doing?"

"I came to see who this sexy man you're keeping to yourself is, silly." Janelle held out her arm, wrist limp, breasts thrust out, and smiled at Brady. "Janelle Langdon. Supermodel. *Sports Illustrated*, page twenty-three. This year's edition."

Brady gravitated toward Janelle, ignoring Crista. "It's a pleasure. I'm … "

Crista walked away. Not interested in being the third wheel or competing with Janelle, she wanted to hunt down Bruce. He obviously wasn't with Janelle. She only hoped he hadn't abandoned her and gone home.

She found him holding two glasses of champagne by the doors open to the outside gardens. His brow pulled down and his mouth set in a firm line when he caught sight of her. She marched straight toward him, took one of the flutes out of his hand, and drank.

"Thanks for abandoning me." She studied him, but his eyes followed Janelle on the dance floor. "This isn't working. She stole the guy who asked me to dance. You need to go break them up … feel free to trip Brady and put a shoe up his ass for ignoring me too, if you want."

"I tried." He raised his glass and shot the whole thing back in one swallow.

The visual of Bruce going after Brady tickled her bad mood. She grinned. "You tripped him?"

"Huh?" Bruce shook his head. "No, you're right. This isn't working. Janelle shot me down when I asked her to dance."

"Well, Brady seemed to do nothing special to get her attention." She sounded bitchy, even to her own ears.

Bruce's lip curled. "I hate dancing."

"It's not my favorite thing to do either, especially in this dress," she said.

He finally looked over at her. "You do look nice. I don't know what you're complaining about."

"Not supermodel nice though. Janelle gave one look to Brady, and he was all over her; I wasn't even a memory," she muttered. "I can't compete with someone who looks like her. I'm too much of a tomboy."

"No. It's not that." He picked a cracker of caviar off the server's tray as it passed. "You know what I think gets Janelle's juices flowing?"

"Ew." She shuddered. "I'm afraid to find out."

"She's jealous of you." He wiped his mouth with the back of his hand and continued. "She sees you as female competition, not so much as only wanting guys who are attached."

She snorted. "How much have you drank? Have you looked at me?"

"I'm serious." He stepped closer. "She saw you getting attention and didn't want to be outdone. You said she liked a challenge, so let's give her something to fight for. We need to do more than just pretend we're together. Janelle needs to witness us hot and heavy for each other. I need to touch you, whisper to you, connect with you, like I'm *hot* for only you. If she believes I can't control myself around you, she'll push her way between us. And then I got her."

She watched Janelle leave Brady on the floor, looking poleaxed. "Hm. You may be right, but I have a feeling it's about outdoing any female, not just me. Although, I don't think she's picky about the men she goes after. She's just stupid."

"Dammit, we're going to have to dance to make sure she sees us together." He turned around and set his glass on the table, removed her drink from her hand, and got rid of it. "Come on."

"Wait. The music is too fast." She hurried after him, arm bent and pressed to her chest to keep her dress in position, but he wasn't listening.

He swung her around as if casting a line, and she boomeranged back and met his chest. She laughed with her hand permanently attached to the front of the dress. Somehow, she managed to move her body in what she hoped resembled dancing. He gazed at her waist and studiously copied her moves. Stiff and self-conscious, he danced awkwardly. It was the most adorable thing she'd ever seen.

To have him risk his manly reputation by looking klutzy on the dance floor had her respecting him even more. She grew daring, and let go of her dress. If he could push through the discomfort, so could she.

His gaze shifted to her face and he flashed her a smile. A smile she knew sent most women to panting after him. Janelle seriously needed to consult a therapist over her taste in men because her available man radar was off the mark. Bruce was too good for someone so shallow.

She moved in closer, grabbed his hips, and got them moving in the same direction as hers. He put his hands on the sides of her ribs, and she raised her hands, gyrating to the beat. He gave her dress a tug, keeping it in place.

She laughed, letting loose. "Don't let it slip."

"I got your back … er, your front," he said with a wink.

The music changed to a slower, more sedate song. She moved toward him naturally, laying her head on his chest. She sighed. "You're really not that bad of dancer. You only need to do it more often, so you loosen up."

"Right. I'll start tomorrow." He grunted, belying his words. "Tell you the truth. You're the only woman I've danced with that I can remember. Once at Grayson and Shauna's wedding when they asked us to start the dancing part of the reception, and now here."

An alien pang of possessive feelings hit her. She liked the thought of being the only woman who danced with him. She longed to be someone's special something, and she had no memories of being someone's *only* anything until now. Even though the special moment was with Bruce, the intimacy of being a part of his memory pleased her.

He was a huge part of her life, and she couldn't imagine life without him by her side. Her chest warmed. He meant the world to her.

He'd asked her yesterday if she ever thought she'd get married. The question had surprised her because no one had ever asked her that before. Interview questions were always based on her stamina, training, and goals for the next Ironman.

The truth was she thought about marriage more than she wanted to admit. Intense training was hard on a woman's body. She was no exception, and she worried that competing too long at a level that might rob her of eventually being capable of having a family would push her dreams to the side. At twenty-seven years old, she secretly stressed about if marriage and having children were in her immediate future. Her desire to have two point five children and a husband who loved her more than anything called to her as much as winning the next Ironman.

"Crista, darling." Janelle's voice came from behind her.

She groaned and lifted her head off Bruce's chest, finding her nemesis ready to pounce. "Yes?"

"Your boyfriend asked me earlier if I wanted to dance when you were otherwise unavailable, and I'm here to take him up on the offer." She pushed Crista's arm gently. "You'll excuse us, won't you?"

She glanced at Bruce, who looked at Janelle. "Sure. Knock yourself out."

For a few minutes in Bruce's arms, she'd allowed herself to have a good time with him. Then Janelle splashed her with the dose of reality. She wasn't here with Bruce. Her job was to make Janelle jealous. It sucked to be a best friend.

Chapter Four

On the dance floor, Janelle's hips went one way and her breasts went the other. Bruce locked his gaze on those hips, and tried to move in a manner where it looked like he was dancing. Unlike Crista who'd helped him look halfway cool and confident while dancing, Janelle wasn't helping him out.

Janelle moved around him, against him, and kept his body in one place as if he were her personal stripper pole, and she the star at a bachelor party. The curve of her ass rubbed against his thigh, and he inhaled sharply. He hooked her waist, bringing her tight against him. She was ready to go and he'd rather not waste time dancing.

"Why don't we go back to your apartment and continue this dance," he said.

Janelle lips swelled in a perfectly formed pout. "What about your girlfriend?"

Bruce glanced over Janelle's shoulder at Crista. His chest tightened. Crista stood in the corner, her left brow raised as she looked at the stem of her glass.

He knew that look. She was either plotting someone's murder or having dirty thoughts. Energy swelled in his chest and he grew agitated. He wanted to know what she was thinking. Usually, he was the one egging her on—whether to go dirtier or to get in trouble—he didn't care because she was fun to hang out with, and the opportunity to egg her on was prime. Normally, she'd blame him when she got in trouble or blushed so her cheeks matched the pink stripe in her hair whenever he convinced her to tell him what naughty thought were going through her head.

Would she mind if he took off with Janelle? He didn't want to leave her alone at the party.

A man in a suit approached Crista. She smiled and moved away, leaving the guy watching her. Bruce grimaced for the poor guy. Crista never played games and always came off as stuck up instead of simply clueless about how normal females were supposed to respond.

She had no idea half the men in the room were watching her. He stepped to the side to keep Crista in sight, but Janelle stopped him.

"Well?" Janelle trailed her finger along the collar of his shirt.

He turned his attention back to Janelle. "What?"

"Crista? Is she going to start trouble if you go home with me instead of her?" Janelle asked.

"Ah … " He glanced back to where Crista was standing, but she was gone. "No. I'll talk to her so she understands. Don't worry."

Where the hell did she go?

"Excellent." Janelle wound her arm around his waist. "Let's make it an early night and go back to my apartment."

"Sure, baby." He removed her arm. "Let me get things squared away with Crista and find her a way home, since we came together. Then I'll take care of you."

Janelle folded her arms, which accented her breasts even more. He moistened his lips. Damn, those babies were about ready to burst. As fast as lust hit him below the belt, disappointment swept through him. He'd had all kinds of breasts. Flat, overflowing, firm, soft, and saline. Fake boobs always came in on the bottom of his sexual totem pole.

"Hang on. I'll go tell Crista I'm leaving." He dragged his gaze away and went to find his "date." In a couple of hours, he'd have Janelle hooked and bagged. His vacation would be fulfilled, and he'd go back home more relaxed.

Three men stood by the refreshment bar where he'd last seen Crista. He approached them. "Have you seen a woman, about this high—" he held his hand up to his chest "—dark hair with a pink stripe, wearing a white dress?"

The man with a buzz cut and a tattoo peeking out of the collar of his tux grinned. "Seen her? Oh yeah. Hot chick."

"She had a tight ass." The dark-haired guy whistled. "Must be a model because she was smokin'."

"She's not a model." Bruce lowered his voice. "If she comes back here, can you let her know I'm … never mind."

He scanned the room again, and not finding her, he pushed through the double doors to the patio. Couples lounged around in the wrought iron chairs and stood beside the over-the-top fountain with a naked woman spraying water out her mouth. He thought the statue looked a lot like Crista. He shook his head and looked away. Nah, the damn thing was a mermaid.

Familiar feminine laughter came from the other side of the fountain. Bruce walked around the perimeter, keeping his gaze off Cri—the mermaid statue's voluptuous breasts.

He found Crista sitting on the raised cement seat at the edge of the water. Two men were standing in front of her, hands in pockets, and rocking back on the heels of their leather shoes in amusement. He stopped a few feet away. Something wasn't right.

Crista almost sounded as if she were flirting with the two men. Her laugh was higher than normal, yet softer, too. His muscles tensed. She'd never made that sound with him before.

She kept pressing her slim fingers to her collarbone. He glanced at the men. Yep, they were following her hand and getting their fill of her breasts. He clenched his teeth when it finally dawned on him she was drunk.

She rarely drank, and when she did, she wasn't one of those women who giggled and entertained men. Irritated that he could be with Janelle back at her apartment right now, settled between her long, lean legs, he was babysitting Crista instead. Realizing he couldn't leave her here in her condition, he moved forward.

Crista leaned back and removed her hand from her *bare* chest as she laughed, kicking her *bare* leg out in front of her, where her high heel tottered on the end of her *bare* foot. He clamped his teeth together because he'd bought her the dress that barely covered her. Hell, she was practically naked! He hadn't noticed that earlier when she'd complained about the dress not being right for her.

He strode in front of her and looked at the two men. No, he *glared* at the two men. He wasn't going to let them take advantage of her carefree spirit and her lack of judgment. Following an unspoken universal sign that meant *back the fuck off*, the two men said their goodbyes and strolled away.

Crista tugged on his pant leg. "I take it you struck out, huh?"

He turned his attention to her and frowned. "No, I didn't strike out. But because I have to take you home, I can kiss my free ticket to Janelle goodbye."

"What are you talking about?" She uncrossed her legs and stood in front of him. "Go be with her if you want. I'm not stopping you."

"You're drunk. I'm not leaving you here to get into trouble." He searched for her glass to dump the rest of the drink out and couldn't find it.

"I'm not drunk." She planted her hands on his chest and shoved. "I took a couple sips and didn't even finish my champagne. Where did you get that stupid idea?"

"Look at you … " He pointed at her, waving his hand up and down. "You were laughing and smiling at those men. Strangers, might I add, and acting like you weren't in control of yourself. All you're doing is asking for trouble. You have no idea what goes through a man's head when he sees someone who looks like you."

Crista's mouth came open and she blinked up at him, speechless. He scoffed and let his head fall back as he took in the lights surrounding the patio. Why was he arguing with her?

She could do anything she wanted, and he was a guest at her house. He blew out his breath. Going without sex was affecting his thinking.

He had no say in Crista's life or who she talked with or how she acted or what choices she made.

"Listen." He gazed at her again. "I'm sorry. I just never saw you … doing *that* before."

Crista tugged her dress up. "Doing what?"

He eyed her breasts, surprised when they swelled and ballooned over the top when she adjusted the top of the material. He rubbed the back of his neck, unable to look away. He knew they were real, but when was the last time he'd seen her like *that*, wearing *that*, and showing off *those*?

"Well?" She cocked her hip and planted her hands at her waist.

"Jet lag," he muttered, latching onto a plausible excuse for his reaction. "I'm ready to get out of here. You?"

Her shoulders sagged and she stepped closer. "Finally. Let's go home."

It wasn't something he planned, but somehow he found himself following her back inside the beach house and across the main room. His cock hardened halfway to the door. She had a hell of a walk; her tight ass and loose hips were the perfect combination.

Unprepared for such a reaction, he had to do something because the last thing he needed was to think of Crista as … hell, he couldn't go there. She was his best friend. They'd done everything together. They laughed, fought, conspired, and supported each other. He hurried forward and opened the door, letting her go under his arm and outside first.

The door shut and he held her arm as she navigated the steps in her heels. Her smooth skin felt nice under his fingers and he moved his hand higher.

She glanced at him. "Are you all right?"

"Yeah." He shrugged off her concern. He'd be perfect once he had sex. Tonight proved he was past lucid thoughts and was hallucinating. Crista was off limits and his best friend. Hell, she might as well be his sister for how well he knew her.

He shuddered. At least he called that tremble that swept down his spine and landed in his balls a sign of repulsion. He only went out with girls like Janelle who were unattached to him emotionally, and who he wouldn't have to see after they were done having sex. He went for low maintenance and no obligation sex, not girlfriends or relationships.

"Bruce … Crista," a woman's voice called out behind him.

Crista groaned. He glanced over his shoulder, and he wanted to groan, too. There, hurrying down the steps of the house was his sure deal—the in his pocket, free sex for the night woman coming right toward them, and she did not look thrilled to see him leaving with Crista.

"You two are leaving?" Janelle directed her question at Bruce.

Crista yawned. Janelle snapped her attention to Crista and glared as if the whole night was her fault. This was a disaster waiting to happen, and there was only one thing he could do to stop trouble before it started. He had to continue playing the part of Crista's boyfriend and keep Janelle interested and hanging in there a little longer.

He looped his arm across Crista's shoulders, pulling her to his side. Her hand went to his stomach out of surprise but provided the perfect sign of them having an intimate relationship. "Do you need a ride home? We have room if you'd like to go with us back to the apartments," he said.

Janelle's lips pursed and she glared even more. He could barely view the shocking blue color of her eyes through the barrier of false black eyelashes. He glanced down at Crista, who gazed up at him.

Crista's serious expression belied her amusement because her bright green eyes fairly danced with laughter. He tightened his hold on her and hoped for once she didn't do something that would have him busting a gut. "Isn't that right, sweetheart?"

"Sure." Crista smiled at Janelle. "My car has a comfortable backseat … lots of leg room for a sports car."

Janelle pivoted without answering, marched back into the house, and finally let her opinion of them be known when she slammed the oversized, solid wood door with the brass handle. Bruce winced. "I guess she has another way home."

"Appears that way," Crista said. "Bummer."

He looked at her. She looked at him. They both burst out laughing and didn't stop until they were pulling into the parking garage at Crista's apartment. He was okay with that because somewhere between the party and Crista's place, he decided he really didn't want to expend the energy it would take to get Janelle into bed.

Chapter Five

The iron clank of the barbell hitting the stand echoed in the weight room. Crista sat up from her spot on the bench, wiping the stray strands of hair off her overheated face. If she hadn't eaten an onion burger and fries last night with Bruce, she could've cut her workout in half. As it was, she'd probably still gained five unwanted pounds.

"Done?" Bruce let the leg machine slowly retract back in place and planted his feet on the floor.

"Yep." Crista stood. "Are you up to ten miles on the bike?"

Bruce eyed the exercise bicycle in front of the mirror. "Staring at myself while being stationary isn't my favorite thing to do."

"Yeah, well, I was talking about riding outside on two wheels that actually propel you forward." She laughed. "It does a body good."

Bruce clicked his tongue and shook his head. "Still not feeling it. The last time I went bicycling with you, I had the bike seat impression in the crack of my ass for a month. Let's just say, it wasn't an enjoyable experience."

"Crude, dude." Crista sniffed and wrinkled her nose. "I need a shower."

"Yeah, me, too." He grabbed his towel and wiped his face, looping the material around his neck. "How about we hit the beach afterward instead of the self-punishment of the bicycle seat?"

"Sounds good." She pushed through the door and walked into the hallway. "Don't forget that Grayson and Shauna are coming over tomorrow. We need to plan a night out that's baby friendly."

Bruce pushed the elevator button. "How would I know where it's safe to take a kid?"

"You expect me to know just because I'm a woman?" Crista nudged him with her elbow. "You probably expect a woman to be barefoot and in dresses when you get home from earning all the money, huh?"

"It's a fantasy." He stepped inside the elevator and held the door open for her. "Don't you want kids someday?"

Her stomach flip-flopped. His question hit too close to home. She hadn't talked with anyone about her desires to slow down, ease up on training, and think about settling down. Most women, she suspected, only thought about their future after they were in a serious relationship. She worked in reverse order, and since she needed a man to give her a baby, her chances were slim.

"I do," she said, clearing her throat to ask louder. "Don't you? Someday, I mean?"

"Sure. I think all men do. It's in my body to procreate and want to see little Bruce Juniors running around and hitting the cover of *Sports Illustrated* or *Bass Angler*," he said.

She opened her mouth to ask him when he planned on settling down, when a slim arm slipped between the closing elevator door, distracting her. She stepped back against the rail, staring at the blood red fingernails as they curled around the door, stopping the elevator from closing. She sagged against the wall and held on to the rail for support.

The door changed directions and Janelle came into view. Irritated over being interrupted just when she was about to get some information about where Bruce was in his life, she scooted closer to her friend, hoping Janelle would take the hint and get lost. As soon as Janelle stepped inside and hit the third floor button, she turned on Crista.

"You're not answering your cell phone," Janelle stated.

She held her hands, palms up, letting Janelle see the bicycle shorts and sports bra were the only things she had on. "When I'm training, I never carry a phone."

Janelle leaned against the wall, cupped her elbow with one hand, and delicately fanned the air under her nose. "I can tell you're exercising."

"Really?" Crista stepped forward, but Bruce planted his hand flat in the middle of her stomach to keep her away from Janelle.

Anger rolled over her. She shrugged Bruce away, but his hand only moved to the back of her and held the waist of her shorts. She was tired of Janelle.

All the attitude and demeaning comments had taken their toll, and she was done. She inhaled through her nose and curled her fingers into fists. Her problem with Janelle wasn't only the lack of respect she received. She was also tired of feeling like Janelle's ugly stepsister.

"Whatever." Janelle's gaze finally landed on Bruce. "You're looking hot, Bruce."

The model's gaze lowered and her finely shaped brow arched at the sight of Bruce's loose sweat pants hanging from his hips. Crista rolled her eyes as the elevator dinged.

Without waiting a second, she charged out and headed toward her apartment. It wasn't until she was at the door punching in the code that she realized Bruce wasn't with her. She peered down the empty hallway, looked at the closed door to Janelle's apartment and snorted.

"That bitch," she muttered.

Stinky, pissed, and feeling kinship to a warty frog, she entered her apartment and headed to the shower. If Bruce wanted to ruin his life getting hooked up with Janelle, then he was on his own. She wasn't going to help him anymore.

While she showered, she stewed. It wasn't as if Janelle was better than her. Janelle had a more active social life, but Crista wasn't looking to bed-hop and fill her life with meaningless friendships. Janelle reminded her of an immature eighteen-year old who suddenly walked out of a strict upbringing and wanted to experience everything at once, no matter what her actions did to everyone else. Crista was past that.

She stepped out of the shower and dried off, leaving her hair wet and dripping. She was also frustrated because Bruce was making a fool of himself by playing Janelle's game just to get sex and prove he was man enough to bag the supermodel. His behavior was pathetic because all he saw in Janelle was a good lay. Crista tossed the towel in the hamper and paused. Fine, if she wanted to be honest, she was jealous that Bruce seemed to fawn over someone totally unlike her.

Ever since she was fourteen, she'd trained and made her life all about competing in marathons, triathlons, and the Ironman. She was proud of what she'd accomplished, but she'd be the first to admit that she'd missed out on a lot of normal things. It was only natural that she'd compare her sex life with Janelle's and come away feeling like the loser out of the two.

She slapped the hamper closed. Now she was too old to act stupid around a man, go out, get drunk, and dance on a table. Everyone knew her, and if they didn't know her for what she'd gained through hard work and dedication, they remembered that silly shot of her running out of the ocean in a bikini that *did* make the cover of *Sports Illustrated*.

Sure, it wasn't the swimsuit addition and she'd had sand in her ass and her hair in a swimcap, but she'd heard the talk. Not everyone thought she was hideous.

She sighed, opened the bathroom door, and walked out naked to get dressed in her room. From now on, she was going to cut off her relationship with Janelle. Toxic friendships messed with her head, and she needed to concentrate on getting in the best shape she could so she could step away from her career on a win.

In the hall, she picked up the dirty towel on the floor and stared at it. It wasn't one of hers.

The spare bedroom door opened. She dropped the towel in surprise and stared at Bruce. He was supposed to be with Janelle.

Bruce's gaze dropped to her bare breasts. Heat rose to the surface of her skin. She stood naked in front of him with nothing in her hands to hide behind. As quickly as that thought passed through her head, she also came to the conclusion that he wasn't with Janelle, and she'd be damned if she was going to cower in embarrassment because she was more mature, more confident, and more secure than her next door neighbor.

Bare chested and wearing only a pair of jeans, Bruce continued to soak in every little detail of her body. His gaze went from her breasts to her legs and back again. His mouth softened and he leaned against the doorframe as if he had all the time in the world to look at his best friend. Her pulse raced. Unable to stop her reaction from his intense inspection, her nipples peaked and warmth spread throughout her body, congregating between her legs.

The feelings were so alien to her, she grew lightheaded. She shouldn't feel … what? She swallowed hard. Turned on? Pleased? Powerful? Sexy?

She moved forward to slip into her room to escape the uncomfortable situation, and Bruce stepped into her path. Standing inches away from him, she smelled the soap from his shower. She quivered because it was the most intoxicating scent she'd encountered coming off his warm body.

"I—I thought you were—"

He hooked her neck, dragging her forward, and kissed her hard. Shocked and unprepared, she could only let him. The taste of him penetrated her numbed thoughts, and she opened her mouth. Bruce took that as an invitation. She moaned at the swipe of his tongue across hers. The warmth, the heady taste of toothpaste and heat, and the urgency coming from him had her kissing him back.

Held captive by this touch, she placed her hands on his sides. The hardness radiating off his body broke through all her inhibitions. She explored his ribs, his sides, his hips, marveling at the tone, the heat, the sculpted body. Somewhere deep inside of her pulsed, and she closed her eyes, willing the feelings to stay. She forgot whom she was kissing and what he was doing to her.

All she wanted was more.

And she wanted that something now.

Bruce tilted her head to the side and deepened the kiss. Her legs wobbled and she practically lay in the crook of his arm. His other hand came up and cupped the curve of her breast. She shifted, giving him access, and when his thumb swept over her sensitive nipple, the most wonderful burst of pleasure flooded her sex.

His hardness pressed against her. She clung to him, afraid she'd collapse in a heap at his feet if he let go or stopped. His tongue tangled with hers, licking, sucking, nibbling. She pressed her breasts into his palm and he squeezed.

Lightheaded and consumed with needing him, she stumbled back a step when he removed his hands. She panted, out of breath, confused over what had happened to make him kiss her, for her to kiss him back, and not want him to stop.

"Why did you—"

He ran his hands over his bare chest, gathering his own lost breath. "Doorbell."

"What?" She shivered, lost without his heat.

He gazed at her and she saw reality come crashing down on him. She turned away, crossing her arms. Her nakedness no longer felt good. Her throat closed in fear that what had happened between them would forever change their relationship.

The doorbell rang. She flinched.

"I'll get it. You can go get dressed." He stepped around her, avoiding touching her.

She swallowed her regrets and walked into the bedroom. Behind the closed door, she sat on the edge of the bed, pulling the throw blanket over her shoulders and bending at the waist until she cradled her head in her hands. What had she done?

She'd kissed Bruce. Granted, he'd made the first move and kissed her first, but he was her best friend. She closed her eyes and groaned. This was not good.

Chapter Six

The gulls flew overhead as the surf washed up on shore, promising the birds a treat. Bruce stared out at the waves. The hypnotic movements usually put him at peace, but today they only made time go slower.

He'd left the apartment at sunrise to run along the beach, trying to keep busy while Crista slept. She'd skipped out of the apartment yesterday while Janelle—who'd shut him down the moment he stepped out of the elevator and into her apartment, waving him off as if he wasn't the guy who never struck out with women—had interrupted his kiss with Crista and tried to convince him to go back to her apartment with him. The fact that the woman had approached him when he was getting it on with Crista had nothing to do with his anger. He hated the way she had no respect for his best friend. To skank in front of a man's woman—even if it was a ruse and he and Crista were not really together—was low in his book.

Besides, Janelle had her chance when he walked into her apartment and sent Crista home alone. Why had Janelle changed her mind the moment she closed the door? There was no reason to come looking for him, and he didn't believe her excuse that she'd had a headache earlier but now wanted to pick things up by inviting him back to her apartment.

Despite her great body, Janelle's personality killed any desire to have sex with her. She was materialistic, high maintenance, and he wouldn't tolerate anyone who talked about Crista the way she had yesterday.

Before he could right the situation, Crista left the apartment without so much as looking at him or Janelle. He'd tried to stop her, but Janelle blocked him from going out the door. Then when he'd called her cell to have her come back, the damn phone rang in her room. He heard her come back in at ten o'clock that night, carrying her bike into the apartment and putting it on the patio. He'd lain awake, thinking she'd come in and talk with him before she retired to her own room the way she always did, but her door shut and the lock clicked into place.

Not once had Crista locked her door on him.

He picked up his shoes and headed back to the apartment. Hopefully, Crista would be fully awake, and he could explain what had happened between them yesterday. Hell, he wasn't sure what happened when he kissed her.

The passion he'd felt wasn't planned. He equated the kiss with getting slapped upside the head by a low-lying branch when fishing the shoreline. Shocked and knocked loopy, all he could do was embrace the best thing he'd ever experienced. He'd tell her the truth. He hadn't been thinking. He had no plans beyond that kiss, and he'd apologize. Apologizing was good. Women loved to know he was wrong and they were right. Crista would laugh over his lapse in judgment, and they'd go back to being friends. Hell, maybe it'd be better if he called his vacation short and flew out to the cabin for a few days. The way his track record was going, solitude would do wonders for him.

His biorhythm or some other kind of shit Crista was always talking about must be off kilter. He'd never had so much trouble with women before.

Or, he could take Janelle up on her offer and prove that the kiss he'd shared with Crista was nothing more than a weak moment in his life. Everything would go back to being normal, and he'd have his best friend back. Then they could both stop wigging out about their shared kiss. He kicked at the sand. Shit.

He no longer wanted Janelle. He couldn't even come up with one reason why he'd wanted her in the first place. What was he supposed to do?

He walked up the stairs out of the sand, across the boardwalk, and keyed in the entrance code to the building. At the door to the apartment, he blew out his breath. He hoped Crista was in a good mood and would forgive him.

He walked inside, and Crista whirled around with a smile on her face. He set down his shoes, glad to see they were back on friendly terms.

"Hey," he said.

Her smile faded and she looked away, busying herself folding clothes on the couch. "Hey. Grayson called, they're about five minutes away. I thought you were him."

He ran his hands through his hair, surprised it was already dry from using one of the outdoor showers on the beach after his run. He must've stayed out longer than he thought.

"I washed your dirty laundry and folded the clothes." She shoved a stack of shirts at him. "There's a bran muffin on the counter and some oatmeal in a bowl on the top shelf in the refrigerator. All you have to do is put it in the microwave for ninety seconds. There's milk and honey, too."

"Thanks, but I'm good." He set the clothes down on the coffee table and grabbed her wrist. "Hey, can you talk with me for a second … "

She flinched and her body went stiff. "Grayson and Shauna will be here any minute. I need to put things away and make sure everything is out of Trevor's reach ."

"I need to talk to you." He let her go. "About yesterday."

She waved him off. "No big deal. It was nothing."

"I wouldn't exactly say it was nothing," he muttered. "We kissed."

She wrinkled her nose at the same time the doorbell rang. "They're here. Hurry, put your clothes away, and don't say a word about … you know. Nobody needs to know what happened, especially Shauna. She'll blow it all out of proportion, and we both know it was nothing."

Nothing?

It was a hell of a lot more than nothing. Nothing was kissing her with a closed mouth on her birthday. Nothing wasn't even part of the equation when he had his tongue shoved in her mouth and a hand cupped over her breast. His gaze followed Crista across the room. She wasn't wearing a sports bra today. How come he hadn't noticed how plump her breasts were before now?

She had a slim, tight body, muscled and contoured. Yet, there was nothing about her breasts that hinted at muscle. Those beautiful globes were soft, free moving, and right there for him to enjoy.

"Get the door, Bruce." Crista slipped into the hallway, disappearing from view.

He glanced down at the front of his sweats, adjusted himself, and went over and let his friends in.

"Coldwell." Grayson removed his arm from around Shauna's shoulders and shook Bruce's hand. "How's the vacation going?"

Grayson, past Wimbledon tennis champion, current owner of Schyler's Tennis Center, and one of his good friends had remained a constant in his life ever since they met years ago at a celebrity dinner. He'd married Shauna, who'd grown up stalking the athlete, and lived a good life in Cottage Grove, California.

"Decent." He grinned at Grayson before leaning over and kissing Shauna's cheek. "Hey, gorgeous. How's mommyhood treating you?"

Shauna smiled and the absolute contentment was contagious. "Trevor slept all night, and I've realized eight hours of sleep is better than any vacation."

Two-year-old Trevor used that moment to launch himself in Bruce's direction. Shauna laughed. "I think he remembers you."

She thrust the kid at him. "Here you go, baby, time for some male bonding with your Uncle Bruce."

Bruce scrambled to keep from dropping Trevor. He gazed down at Grayson and Shauna's son. The blond hair, blue eyes, and outgoing spirit captured the best of both his parents. The town of Cottage Grove better be ready when this kid grew up.

"You made it," Crista said. "Welcome to southern Cali. Only a hop and skip from northern Cali."

"I know." Shauna inhaled deeply. "We don't get down this way often enough, but we're here."

Crista hugged everyone but Bruce and then stood beside him, holding Trevor's hand and making cooing noises at the boy. Bruce checked her out while she was distracted. She'd changed clothes while in the bedroom and brushed her hair.

The white tank showed off her tan, and the mini-mini-mini skirt hugged her body. He leaned over, dipping Trevor in a playful game of *whee, I'm going to drop you, aren't you a lucky kid* and used the movement to ogle Crista's legs.

"More, more." Trevor giggled.

Bruce straightened, coming up and having three sets of eyes on him with matched expressions of confusion—except Grayson who slowly grinned. Guilt flashed through him at getting caught looking at Crista's legs. He glanced at Crista and Shauna, who stared back at him as if he'd made a social blunder. "What?"

"Girl time." Shauna tugged a shocked Crista into the living room.

Grayson stepped over into the kitchen and leaned against the counter. "So … ?"

Hooked and tossed up on the sand like an undersized fish, Bruce did the only thing he could. He changed the subject. "How's the tennis center doing?"

"Good." Grayson rubbed his hand across his jawline. "What's up with you and Crista?"

"I've been staying with her before I have to head out next week."
Bruce put Trevor on the floor, looked around for something to
give the kid, and found the muffin Crista left him for breakfast.
He held it up for Grayson's okay, and with his approval, he gave
the boy the food.

Trevor held the muffin in the air and ran off into the living
room. Bruce sagged in relief.

"I doubt if Crista wants him eating all over her apartment,"
Grayson said. "He hasn't learned how to contain the messes he
makes yet."

Bruce blew out his cheeks. He couldn't do anything right. The
kiss with Crista was a huge mistake. Looking at his best friend in
front of his other friends was a mistake. Even feeding an innocent
kid a healthy snack was a mistake. Until he could straighten out
his problems with Crista, he was on a capsized boat and going
under.

"Since you're ignoring my question, let's make this simple."
Grayson crossed his arms over his chest. "Do you have the hots
for Crista?"

"You mean as a man and a woman have the hots for each
other?" Bruce shook his head. "No, of course not."

"Did something happen between you two?" Grayson continued.

"No … yes." He tapped his fist on the counter. "It was nothing."

Nothing? He was an ass. Crista told him as much earlier, but
it wasn't true. It was the best damn kiss he'd ever had. The longer
Crista kept believing it was a mistake, the more pissed off he was
getting.

"I fucked up," he whispered. "Last night, I kissed her. I'm not
talking any old kiss, we were having sex."

"With Crista?" Grayson whistled softly. "Sex with Crista … "

"No, not sex. Her mouth was that damn good it might as well
have been sex," he said.

Grayson chuckled. "A little advice, bro to bro. Don't fuck with her, man. I've been there, you've been there, and it's not worth it. Tell her the truth about how you're feeling and what she means to you. If you're serious about Crista, being upfront right from the beginning will save you a lifetime of hell."

That's what he'd do when Crista decided to finally speak to him about what happened yesterday. He nodded. "I'm serious … more serious than I've ever been. I'm trying to do the right thing, but she keeps changing the subject, and then you guys showed up. I haven't had time to straighten things out between us."

"Sorry." Grayson chuckled, not a bit apologetic. "After the girls talk, we're planning on heading up to San Jose to see Dominic for dinner. It's a quick trip this time around because I have a crew coming into the center for an interview."

"Another tournament?" he asked.

Grayson shook his head. "It's for Shauna. She's hosting a gala for the senator next month."

"I can't believe how far she's come. Ever since her success with the fundraiser at Cottage Grove, she's put on some huge events." Bruce slapped his hand on Grayson's shoulder. "I envy you your family. That's what it's all about. A good woman who loves you. A son. Success. Wimbledon status. Retirement in the bag. Not to mention sex whenever you want it. I want to be you, bro."

Grayson's lip twitched and he lifted his chin, motioning behind Bruce. He glanced over his shoulder at Crista, holding Trevor, and Shauna. Going by Crista's imitation of an endangered spotted owl in an Oregon forest and Shauna's crinkled eyes as she tried unsuccessfully to hide her amusement, Bruce concluded that both of them heard what he'd said to Grayson.

"Just pumping him up and making him feel better." Bruce winked at Shauna, trying to save his reputation.

Crista continued to stare at him without making any comments. At a loss for words, he stood there and looked back at Crista, willing her to understand. But how could she when he didn't even understand what he was talking about?

Eventually, Trevor broke the awkward silence when he squirmed to get down and Crista looked away.

"Go." Trevor caught himself when he tripped over the rug in the kitchen and headed straight to Bruce. "Go."

Bruce laughed and Trevor wrapped his arms around his leg and sat down on his foot. "You remember, huh?"

Two months ago, he'd shown Trevor how to sit on his boot and then proceeded to take him on a ride. To keep him entertained at the Schylers' party, he walked around with Trevor glued to his leg. He felt like an idiot at the time, especially when his leg needed a rest after awhile. But he could hardly tell the little boy to get off because Trevor was not only content but was also giving his parents a needed break.

"Why don't you give him a ride to the elevator? We need to get out of here if we're going to beat the traffic up the coast." Grayson stepped over to Crista. "Sorry we're only dropping in to say hi. We were afraid we wouldn't get to see you before you left for Hawaii, and Shauna thought it was better to have a short visit than no visit at all."

"No, I'm glad you did. I just wish we had more time together, and we, uh, I could take you out to eat and show you the town." She kissed his cheek. "I'll fly to Cottage Grove soon and catch up with you then. The girls are all due for a night out, anyway."

"Sounds like a plan. Bring Bruce along, and I'll call Dominic and Gary. We'll make it a party ... say in a couple of weeks." Grayson stepped back and opened the door. "Get your Uncle Bruce moving, Trev."

Trevor squealed and bounced on Bruce's bare toes. He led the way, feeling stupid but knowing he'd do anything for the kid. No wonder Grayson looked so damn happy. Who could be pissed off at the world when the guy had everything he could want?

Halfway down the hall, Janelle's door opened and she posed in her doorway. Bruce hesitated. Not because he looked forward to another verbal spar with her, but because Crista didn't deserve to have to put up with the girl's shit. He glanced down at Trevor. The kid didn't need to have his Uncle Bruce introduce him to the shadier side of life.

Janelle stuck her nose up at him and smiled in Crista's direction, though her eyes went straight to ogling Grayson. Bruce held his arm out and motioned for them all to keep walking.

"Crista ... I noticed you have more guests visiting." Janelle stepped in front of Shauna, completely ignoring Crista. "I'm Janelle, supermodel for *Sports Illustrated* and the top runway model for Pierre Duponte in Paris."

"Shauna Schyler." Shauna gave her a tight-lipped smile. "Nice to meet you."

Janelle turned her attention to Grayson, but before she could take one step toward him, Shauna blocked her way. "I don't think so."

Janelle batted her lashes. "Excuse me?"

"Back off." Shauna glanced behind her at Grayson. "Honey, can you get *our son* and I'll meet you at the elevator?"

Grayson smacked Shauna's ass as he walked by and whispered loud enough everyone heard him, "That's hot, baby."

Crista bit down on her bottom lip to keep from laughing, and the sight of her happy warmed Bruce's chest. He scooped up Trevor and passed him to his dad. He not only wanted to find the contentment Grayson had found in his life, but he'd also pay big money to see Crista go toe-to-toe with Janelle the way Shauna had.

He glanced behind him at the girls, who stood facing each other off. Crista tugged on Shauna's arm and whispered something to her. Bruce turned back around. For some reason, Crista backed off from confronting Janelle, even with Shauna there as back up. It was long past time she put a stop to Janelle being a bitch to her.

Crista's lack of confrontation when it came to Janelle bothered him. What stopped her from standing up to Janelle if the bitch made her miserable?

Chapter Seven

Between the training class Crista was teaching and Bruce running down to Cabella's to autograph fishing poles to sell to the customers, he hadn't had time to talk to her in the two days since Grayson and Shauna's visit. He'd tried, but Crista kept the few minutes they had together before running in different directions all about what food was in the fridge and occasionally kidding him about cleaning the bathroom while she was gone.

His frustration level exceeded anything he'd ever experienced. Even disasters during a fishing tournament bothered him less. At least out on the water, he was in control. In Crista's apartment, he seemed incapable of finding a solution to put their friendship back in order.

He lay on the couch, staring up at the ceiling. Hell, he didn't want to go back to being only friends. He wanted more with Crista. She consumed his thoughts, and his feelings toward her had grown. Looking back, he'd always had his best moments when she was with him. Their kiss had simply multiplied how much he wanted her in his life. Now he wanted more than laughs and companionship. He wanted to experience everything with Crista.

One thing was for sure: if he couldn't kiss Crista again, he'd rather go fishing. Out on the water, he'd be able to clear his mind. He sat up. Hell, that's what he'd do. He had equipment in the rental car. All he needed was a boat.

Pumped to do something to keep his mind off his troubles, he grabbed his cell phone off the coffee table and dialed his friend Allan. Then his answer to his problems hit him. He'd find out if Crista wanted to move forward or if she wanted to remain just friends. If he could get her alone out on the water, she'd focus on him, and he could convince her to give him a shot. Whatever happened, he'd take it because he wasn't going to lose her.

He'd ask Crista to go along with him. No, he'd demand she take the time to go fishing. She'd never be able to tell him no because she always enjoyed going out with him. He'd have her alone, no one around … secluded.

"Hey, Coldwell," Allan said. "It's been a hell of a long time since I talked to you."

"Hey … " He chuckled, hearing Allan's booming voice over the phone. "I know, man. It has been a long time. I have a favor to ask of you."

"Name it," Allan said.

"I'm in town and need to borrow your boat. Just for tonight." Bruce ran his hand through his hair and continued. "Nothing big, just me and a friend."

"Yeah, yeah, sure," Allen said.

Bruce grinned, excited that his plans were falling together. "Great. I owe you."

"Dinner. Next time you're in town." The phone beeped. "Hey, that's Chuck. He's here to take me to the airport. The keys for the boat are tucked inside the left cabinet, bottom drawer. Take care of yourself, and I'll catch you next time, 'kay?"

"Yeah, sure thing. Bye—and thanks." He disconnected the call, tossed his phone in the air, and caught it. "Perfect."

Thirty minutes later, he had a picnic basket—okay, a plastic sack full of food—and the poles and tackle box they'd need in the car. He only needed the girl.

Ten minutes later, Crista came through the door and stopped. He waylaid her by blocking her off from walking down the hallway to her room. "Change your clothes, we're going fishing."

She set down her gym bag. "Now? I just got out of the shower."

"Did you shower at the gym?" He cocked his head. "Why didn't you come up here and shower?"

"Uh … 'cause it's safer." She rolled her eyes.

"Right." He had to get her onto a different subject and stop bringing up what he referred to as their naked kiss. "Great. Then let's go. I have a boat on reserve, and we can spend the rest of the afternoon floating on the water, enjoying ourselves."

"Go ahead and go without me." She squeezed the ends of her damp hair. "I have to … "

He waited for her to finish, but she looked away. "You're avoiding me. I get that, but we're friends. This will be good for both of us. We'll do something normal and get back to not worrying if I'm going to kiss you again."

"Ha! You probably think about it, but it hasn't entered my thoughts. It was nothing, just a kiss. You know you're not the only man I kiss. There are hundreds of men, some I barely know, who I end up kissing." She flounced away. At her bedroom door she said, "Give me five minutes to change."

Yes. He grinned and headed for the door. Not only was he going to go fishing, he was going to prove her wrong. She might've kissed a few men in her life, but she hadn't experienced everything he could do with a kiss.

She was lying—she'd been right there with him when they kissed. He'd had her practically climbing his body. She couldn't deny what they'd done. He'd let her believe her lies and then prove her wrong. First, he had to make sure Crista understood that nothing was going to come between them. Not the kiss, not what he planned to do with her in the future, and definitely not Janelle. From now on, Crista got all his attention.

A half hour later, he escorted Crista onto Allan's yacht. He made quick work of untying the boat from the dock and setting the course out into the Pacific Ocean. The tide was going out, and they cruised over the barrier and hit smooth water fifteen minutes out. He stretched his shoulders, reveling in the ease of his muscles now that he was out on the water. The weather was perfect to get away from everything.

Seagulls flew overhead and the sun lay low on the horizon, keeping the heat of the day off them. Cool sea mist splashed over the rail as the yacht rocked. He walked over to Crista. Confident and relaxed, he was on his own turf, and he wanted to put her at ease, too.

She held on to the round railing, still struggling to find her sea legs. He stood beside her, enjoying the way she tilted her face to the wind and seemed to enjoy the antics of the birds swarming around the boat, looking for handouts.

Even more than actual fishing today, he wanted to have Crista out here sharing part of his life with him. He loved teaching others about fishing—maybe not ocean fishing, but a line in the water anywhere pleased him. That's why he spent the majority of his free time traveling to different fishing exhibitions and educating others on the newest techniques and equipment from his sponsors.

Crista nudged him with her elbow. "Have you ever thought of living out here?"

"On the ocean?" He shrugged. "I have a boat back home, and it's great for solitude. I don't think I'd want to make it permanent. I need some social activities."

She turned around and leaned against the railing, putting her back to the sea. "I'm like that with training. When I run, I'm in my head. I know most people reach the zone where they can't even remember what thoughts run through their head. I'm the opposite. Doesn't matter if I'm running, biking, or swimming. I'm aware, but nothing bothers me."

He half turned to face her because he wanted to follow the conversation and so far, he was failing. Something had bugged her since he'd arrived, and her subdued attitude had nothing to do with their kiss. "Does it bug you that you're always thinking, planning, reaching for goals?"

She sighed. "Yeah. Sometimes … ," she shrugged. "I don't know. It'd be nice not to think too much. To live each day for whatever reason and not think about tomorrow."

Booyah. Supporting his friend was easy. She finally wanted to talk, and he really wanted to listen.

He pulled her over and wrapped his arms around her. She laid her head on his chest and he placed his hand on her hair. "I know my hugs don't compare to Satchel's, but I'm here for you."

Her arms went around his waist and she said, "You'll do. Sorry I've been such a freak lately."

"Anything I can do?" He rubbed her back.

She rubbed her cheek against his shirt. His balls tightened and he stopped rubbing her body. He waited because he knew what was happening. For once in his life, his brain was working faster than his dick.

Her warm body molded against his. Her breasts smooshed against his stomach, and he swore he could feel her hard nipples, nipples he remembered well, pressing into him. He tilted his head back without letting her go. In fact, he held her tighter.

Ah. Ah. Ah. There it was. He closed his eyes, willing his cock to stand down. She was going to kill him. Today was all about getting back into friend status, not jumping her bones.

Crista wiggled away. "I'm okay now. How about we fish … or you can fish and I can watch."

He wanted to jump for joy, pump the air with his fist, flip off the air. Yes, he was safe. His hard-on would go away, and she'd never know what he was thinking. He'd made it through the first hurdle.

"Yeah, let me get the bait and poles." He walked away, one leg stiffer than the other to hide his erection, and hoped he appeared as if he was walking with the sway of the boat.

He returned to her and with quick efficiency handed her a pole, ready to go in the water. "Let's go to the front, that way our line doesn't come back under the boat."

She followed him and stood at the railing. He laughed at the way she wrinkled her nose at the expired chum on the hook. He'd fished with her before and knew she was game for everything but hooking her own line.

"Think you can cast without hooking yourself?" He looked at her while he threw out his line.

She flipped the tab on the reel, pinched the line with her finger, and proceeded to cast her pole exactly the way he'd taught her years ago. "I only did that once, and we were in a raft. It was hard to stay out of the water, much less keep my balance while casting."

"We've had good times together." He planted his forearms against the railing and leaned over.

Too many hours spent together, relying on each other for support and spilling their guts. She knew everything about him, good and bad. They'd gotten drunk together, they'd been each other's date at friends' weddings, and he even went to her parents' house every few years at Christmas, so she'd have an excuse to get out of there, and vice versa with his parents. His stomach cramped. To think he'd almost blown their friendship because he kissed her made him sick.

What other kind of woman would go out, on the spur of the moment, and go fishing with him? Who'd put up with him crashing at her apartment and voluntarily setting him up with her archenemy? He stared out over the water. His friendship was on the line, and he couldn't lose her.

"Sorry about the other night, sweetheart. You were right. The kiss meant nothing," he said, adjusting his fishing line.

Of course, he was giving her a line of bullshit she needed to hear to keep secure in their relationship. If she couldn't go forward knowing she rocked his world and had him lusting after her every second of the day, he'd lie. He'd lie again and again, if it smoothed things over between them.

Chapter Eight

Nothing?

Nothing?

Crista dug her fingernails into the cork-cushioned handle of the fishing pole. How could Bruce forget how she'd clung to him while they'd kissed? He'd had his tongue in her mouth. She'd felt the proof of his arousal against her. He'd stolen her breath, her dignity, her independence.

Of course she was going to claim it was nothing, but he wasn't supposed to throw that back at her. She swallowed her hurt. It was *something*. A huge something that changed her entire thinking and left her questioning her sanity.

Her stomach rolled and not in a good way. He'd once confessed to getting a hard-on if the wind changed direction. From his stories, she knew better than to go off the signs of a man who was enjoying himself. She glanced over at him and peeked at the front of his jeans. Knowing him, the skank, he was probably getting ready to hump the breeze whipping over the side of the boat.

Only a complete, pathetic loser would think he'd actually enjoyed their kiss. He was a player, a dog, a male bitch. She clamped her lips together. He deserved Janelle and all her baggage.

The reel on Bruce's fishing pole trilled. She glanced over at the same time his line went taut and the pole arched down toward the water.

"That's right … " He jerked up on the pole and set to reeling the fish in. "Got him."

She reeled in her own line and set the pole on the deck. "What do you need, a net?"

"Hook, sweetheart." He motioned his chin. "Right back there on that rigging. Looks like an enormous fishhook, but really heavy, so don't hurt yourself. Pull hard, but be careful, it's sharp."

It took both her hands to pull the piece of equipment out of the wheelie-ma-jig. She tugged and dragged the hook with the cable attached over to the railing and hooked it on the side of the boat, close to Bruce. Then she stood back to watch him bring in the fish. She had no idea what they were trying to catch. It certainly wasn't bass. He'd informed her in the car that bass only came from fresh water, not salt water.

It didn't matter because the only reason she'd agreed to go on a fishing trip with him was because that's what she always did. If he asked, she'd do whatever possible to make sure she helped him. The first time they met, at a media gathering, she'd broken the heel of her shoe walking from the banquet room to the bar across the street from the hotel. Bruce, Dominic, Gary, Juan, and Grayson, who were right behind her when her shoe blew out, stopped and tried to fix her heel. Bruce had finally asked her for her other shoe—and chucked both of them down the alley. He'd then squatted in front of her and told her to hop on his back.

Most men would've carried her back to her room in a gallant show of being a gentleman. She smiled as she watched Bruce talk to himself as he fought with the fish on the other end of the line. No, that night, Bruce gave her a piggyback ride into the bar and planted her ass on the stool. One thing led to another, and they all became best friends … Bruce even more than the other guys.

"All right, you son of a bitch." He rocked back on his heels and groaned through the effort of pulling the fish closer.

She moved toward the railing to peer down into the water. "How big is it? Like the bass you always catch?"

"This is the ocean, sweetheart. This is a halibut." He strained to keep the tip of the fishing pole out of the water. "Real fucking big."

She peered over the railing into the water to see if she could see the fish. "Like the fish and chips kind of fish? Those aren't very big."

"Wait and see." He strained under the pull.

His biceps bulged. She stepped back to get a proper view and wished she hadn't. His tight ass looked good in those jeans. She pulled her gaze away and took in the broad shoulder and thick neck. It wasn't like she was blind to how good looking he was, but she'd never had the time to see him in a different light. That kiss knocked her loopy.

"I need you," Bruce said.

Her mind froze, but her stomach fluttered at his words. She almost swallowed her tongue. "N-need me?"

No one went crazy over their best friend, but she stood in shock, mourning what they could have had together, wanting him, and knowing her life would never be the same because she'd had a taste of him. All because he kissed her.

She wasn't willing to let the possibility of loving him go.

"Sweetheart, you have to move if we're bringing in this fish," he said, snapping her out of realizing she was falling in love with Bruce, or maybe she'd always loved Bruce and needed, no *wanted* more.

"Hurry." He grunted. "As soon as I put the pole in the holder, flip that lock, and move out of the way."

"Okay." She moved into action, doing exactly as he instructed.

Bruce leaned over the side of the boat and a wave rocked him away from the water. She gasped, afraid he'd lose his balance. He situated his legs on the other side of the railing, between the two bottom rungs.

He grabbed the hook from the railing, winked at her with a silly grin, and then pitched head first toward the water. She screamed. Fear paralyzed her. One second he was there, then the next he was gone.

Then his feet, stuck in the railing, moved.

She hurried over to the edge of the boat and peered down. Awe and respect filled her. Instead of him diving over the side into the water, he hung upside down on the side of the boat, hook in hand, and waited for the right moment to catch his fish. Her gaze wandered over the surface of the water. All she saw was the rolling movement of the dark blue sea.

A light grew underneath Bruce in the depth. She shielded her eyes from the setting sun and squealed as the water turned white under the surface and the fish took shape. He was right. The fish must be as big as her sports car.

"Right there." She pointed, jumping up and down. "Holy shit … look at the size of it."

Bruce curled his body, flung the hook, and rolled up until he grasped the railing. She grabbed his shirt, pulling him over into the boat. He instantly moved to hit a button she hadn't noticed on the wall of the yacht, and a whirring noise grew louder, reeling in the cable and hook. She turned toward the railing and watched as the fish—no, a freaking whale of a fish—rose above the water.

"Oh my God." She stood, mesmerized by the size of his catch. She'd never seen a fish the size of the halibut.

Bruce grinned, and his happiness reminded her of all the times she'd witnessed him landing a fish. It didn't matter that this was a different creature than the normal bass that he was known for catching. He was excited and pumped on the catch.

"You're going to have a freezer full of halibut, sweetheart." He laughed.

She could only stand there, shaking her head. No one, especially one person, would be able to eat all the meat. Bruce, in all his he-man, hunt-like-the-savages glory, had taken care of her with a lifetime of fish meat. She melted. He'd always looked out for her, and she'd been too busy to see how much she depended on him.

She swallowed hard. Most times, they teased, competed, and, yes, argued. Half the time she had no understanding how his brain worked, but before now, it hadn't mattered if he had thoughts that she couldn't figure out. She was okay if they had different views and challenged each other to outdo the other when it came to buying gifts for each other. The fact that he bought her something on every trip meant the world to her. He thought of her when they were apart. That had to mean something.

She couldn't imagine a future without him. He wasn't only her best friend, he was everything to her. She wouldn't be happy without him in her life. He wasn't a *want*, but a *need*. She needed him every day to be truly happy because they were more than friends; they were a part of each other's lives.

She sat in the nearest seat and watched Bruce work. Every few minutes, he glanced up at her and smiled, and she melted a little more. She had to tell him what she was thinking, how she was feeling, and get his opinion on whether or not she was absolutely bat-shit crazy to even think that what they'd developed over the years was in fact … love. It was insane, but he was her go-to-guy for all advice, even about whether what she was feeling right at this moment was love.

But she'd have to wait.

She blew out her breath and returned his smile. Fishing came first because she knew him that well. Tonight, she'd spill her guts. Then she'd kiss him. And hopefully he wouldn't say it was nothing.

Chapter Nine

Despite how fast Bruce cut up the halibut, filled her freezer, and delivered a box full of fish to the Fredricksons, an older couple who lived on the first floor of the apartments who Crista knew were on limited income, it was still ten o'clock by the time they called it a night. She plopped down on the chair in the main room, while Bruce collapsed on the couch and yawned. She'd helped, but he'd done the majority of the work because she had no clue what she was doing.

"I bet you're starving," she said.

He rubbed his face and then looked at her. "Nah. Eating the sandwiches on the trip back filled me up. You?"

She shook her head. "I'm good."

She was stalling. The longer she thought about how wonderful and exciting it would be to intimately know Bruce, the more she wanted him. Okay, her neediness was scaring her to death.

Everything about relationships came easy for him because he was a guy. He'd never understand that she was only now seeing him as an available man for the first time. She wanted to share that with him one second and keep the knowledge of her feelings to herself the next second.

God, she was a mess. No wonder he wanted women like Janelle. He went for the girls who had no self-doubt and never hesitated over what they wanted. She couldn't even talk about her feelings. She lacked social skills. If her friends Shauna, Dana, Diana, and Angie were here, they'd know what she should do.

But confiding in them meant Bruce and their whole circle of friends would find out. Then they'd want to get involved. That was the last thing she needed. For her to honestly believe in what Bruce was telling her—if she managed to talk with him—he couldn't have any outside forces pressuring him one way or another.

What she had to do was blurt everything out, and then the awkward subject would no longer be something between them. She glanced at Bruce. He lay there with his arm on his forehead. It was perfect timing. The hour was late, and he'd be unable to make an excuse to go out. Besides, they always did a lot of talking as they both fell asleep.

She had to think of admitting her love for him like a race. For years they'd jogged side by side, no destination in mind, but today she saw a path and if they ran really fast, it'd lead them to a cliff, and if they held hands, they'd fly. She grimaced. With her luck, it was a cliff in the desert and she just got them both killed. She paced the small room. No, she'd visualize a lake, a clear blue lake at the bottom of the cliff.

I can do this.

She sat back down. "Bruce, I need to talk to you and it's pretty wild. Don't interrupt me because this is hard enough as it is, so I'm just going to blurt it all out."

"Okay … " She moistened her lips and swallowed one more time for courage. "Something crazy weird happened when you kissed me—no, I think I was a little freaked out even before you kissed me or I kissed you, I'm not sure who made the first move. You grabbed me, but I was naked, so maybe it was a tie. Anyway, that's beside the point. I think my head got messed up when you started flirting with Janelle or when you asked me to help set you up with her."

Bruce remained lying down, his eyes covered. She inhaled deeply. This was good. He was letting her talk.

"To tell you the truth, I'm starting to think what I'm feeling inside for you was always there. Even clear back when you threw my heels away and hung out with me at the bar, even though

I was the only girl in the establishment with bare feet and way underdressed."

She leaned forward and picked at the hem of her cutoffs. She was going off course. "The thing is, what you don't know is during the last year I've been thinking of my future, a lot. Winning the Ironman for women was great and helped me be noticed by the press and organizations I needed to make contact with to get my name out as a trainer. But my love for what I do has always been about the training, and making other people feel good about themselves, set goals, and realize they, too, can succeed. And well, I want more in my life than a once a year event that'll either make me or break me. I want a boyfriend, a husband, a family. So, I think it's true, for me, I didn't see what was right in front of me this whole time. What's happening now had to happen when I was in the right place in my life for me to recognize it, I suppose. That's where you come in. The other day, I looked up and there you were standing in front of me."

She stood and turned her back to Bruce. Fingering a book on the third shelf on her wall—ironically titled *How to Be a Winner*—she continued. "I don't want you to think I'm settling for you, because you've always been with me as a friend. That kiss … God, that was the most wonderful kiss I've ever had. You touched a part of me that I had no idea I even had. The last couple of days, all I can think about is having your lips on me again, all over me."

Bruce remained quiet. She held her breath and squeezed her eyes shut. She was afraid of turning around and seeing the horror on his face. They always talked about everything but had never approached having feelings for each other. Anxious and scared to death he'd find her repulsive for confessing her feelings toward him, she whirled around, needing to know what he was thinking.

"I need to know if you'll have sex with me?" she said. "I know this isn't romantic and I feel stupid enough as it is, admitting everything to you when you just got done cutting up a fish the size of which I'd never seen before, but it's driving me nuts not telling you all day how I'm feeling, 'cause … well, you're my best friend and I love you. I mean I *love, love* you."

She waited for him to acknowledge his own feelings, or worse, to laugh at her and blame her delusional state on exhaustion making her loopy. Instead, he continued to lie there without responding. She approached the couch, leaned over, and peeked underneath his forearm when a soft snortle came from him, making her jolt. She rocked back a step.

The jerk was asleep.

Bruce lay unaware that she'd had a life changing moment. She folded her arms across the front of her and cupped her elbows. How could he do this to her?

When was she ever going to get up enough nerve to put everything on the line again? She ran her tongue over her teeth. God, they'd spent the last eight hours fishing. She'd taken a quick shower when they got home, but she hadn't brushed her teeth or put makeup on. She wore one of his shirts with a pair of her oldest cutoffs. What if he'd stayed awake and listened, while judging her looks? She was hideous.

She turned and walked out of the room, down the hallway, and closed herself in the bedroom. Not even bothering to get undressed, she lay on the bed and pulled the blanket at the foot of the mattress over her. What the hell was she thinking?

She couldn't compete with Janelle or any of the other beautiful women Bruce was attracted to. She also didn't want to be the aggressor in a relationship because, well, she liked that Bruce had kissed her without her begging him to or letting her reject him.

All she wanted was someone to love her for who she was, maybe sweep her off her feet, and take the responsibility away from her so she could take that jump with him. She closed her eyes. Was it so wrong to want what every other normal woman had?

She groaned. Tonight's outcome was probably for the best. At least Bruce had slept through her embarrassing confession. Because even if he had agreed to have sex, she'd always wonder if he was doing her a favor as her best friend. She needed more. She deserved more.

Chapter Ten

The bedroom door in the back of Crista's apartment shut with a soft click. Bruce removed his arm from his face and stared up at the ceiling, wide awake. His heart raced, and he was sure the thumping of his pulse alone would bring Crista back into the room.

Jesus, shit, and son of a bitch. He opened his mouth and sucked in much needed air.

Once she'd started talking and talking and talking, he was afraid to interrupt her. Then she'd confessed about the opportunity to tell him her feelings were not romantic enough, and he decided to pretend to sleep. She was fucking right.

She deserved romance. To experience being swept off her feet for the first time, and ride the high of discovering love. The whole barrel of fish.

He continued lying there, afraid if he got up, he'd walk straight to her room and take what she offered. Jesus … she wanted to have sex with him.

She'd lied about their kiss. His smile grew and he rubbed his hand across his mouth, trying to wipe it away. He had to make plans. This was huge.

If she wanted romance, he'd damn well give her romance.

Rejuvenated over his epiphany, he watched the clock tick painfully slowly. She'd summed up his mixed feelings and fears every time he thought about her. She was his best friend. Nothing would change that, especially if they were both feeling the same way about each other. He definitely loved her. That was a given. But love-love?

Hell, he didn't even know what love-love was, but he liked the way she'd said the words together, as if they were special and deep.

When an hour passed and he was sure Crista had fallen asleep, he grabbed his cell phone from the counter and slipped out the door. In the hallway of the apartment, he let out the breath he was holding and jogged to the elevator. It wasn't every day a man found out his best friend loved-loved him, and he had to act now.

In the parking garage, he stopped. Glancing around, he declared himself alone and dialed the phone. There was one person who could help him and knew Crista almost as well as he did.

The phone stopped ringing.

"Yes?" Dominic answered.

Hearing the rough Russian accent on the other end of the call further excited him. "Hey, Chekovsky. What's up?"

"Uh … it's after midnight." A groan came over the phone. "What the hell are you doing calling this late, Coldwell?"

"You were asleep?" He walked over to his rental car and sat on the hood. "Sorry, man."

"Not all of us are single and party all night." Dominic whispered to his wife, Diana, and came back to the phone. "Is everything okay? Diana's concerned."

"Yeah, yeah, everything's great." He smacked his forehead with his hand. "Listen, can you go to the john or in another room? I need to talk to you privately, and if Diana overhears, she'll call Crista, and all hell will break lose."

"Sure, I have those hockey scores you want. I wrote them down in the other room. Let me go get them," Dominic said.

"What the hell are you talking about?" he asked.

"Shit." A clatter came over the phone, and then Dominic returned. "Okay, I'm in another part of the condominium. This better be good because Diana will punch me if she catches me lying."

Bruce paused. He was right. Diana, Shauna, Crista, and Juan's wife, Dana, were best friends. Nothing got past the girls, and all his friends knew stealth and downright sneakiness was the only way they could keep anything away from them. "Fine. When we get off the phone, tell Diana I wanted to surprise one of the women in my life, and I needed your help. You won't be lying."

Dominic laughed. "Get real. You never have problems with girls."

"I'm going to tell you something that's going to fucking blow your mind, man." He lowered his voice because although he was alone in the middle of the night in a parking garage, he'd never told a living soul what he was feeling about Crista, and for some reason that left him filled with adrenaline and wanting to shout it to the world. He also knew he should tell Crista first, but he had to try it out on someone else … to be safe … to know if he could even say the words out loud. "I'm falling in love with Crista."

Dead. Silence.

"Uh … " Dominic chuckled. "Do you want me to call for a taxi to come pick you up?"

He dug the heel of his shoe into the bumper of the car. "I'm not drunk. I'm at Crista's … out in the parking garage. Alone … because she wants to have sex with me."

More silence. "Okay, I'm going to hang up and fly over there. Buddy, you need help."

"Dammit. I'm not drinking. I'm not delusional. I don't want to go anywhere, and I sure in the hell don't want you flying over here," he said.

"Are you telling me you want to have sex with Crista?" Dominic asked.

He closed his eyes for a few beats. Dominic was always slow when it came to women. "Yeah, Dominic, I want Crista."

"I … honestly, don't know what to tell you. Are you sure you don't want to talk to Diana about this? She's usually the one who has the best advice when it comes to relationships, and—Crista and you? Seriously?" Dominic said.

His free hand came down and his back straightened. "What do you mean by that?"

"She's our friend," Dominic said. "Hell, she's one of us."

"So?"

"We've all slept with her." Dominic lowered his voice.

"What?" Bruce bellowed, his throat closing up on him.

"You know, when we've shared hotel rooms and crashed during benefit dinners. Not sexual. We're friends. Friends don't have sex. It messes up the universe and brings bad—what does Diana call it—karma or mojo down on you. Maybe you're horny. You should go out and find a different woman. Don't hurt Crista."

He inhaled deeply and held his breath. Dominic understood English, but he wasn't listening to him. He blew out his breath and talked at the same time. "I think I love-love her."

He grimaced. Now he was even starting to sound like Crista.

"I've always loved her as a friend. She's my best friend. We do everything together, but I have to tell you, man, since I came to stay at her apartment, she's changed. I've changed. I can't stop thinking about her. She walks across the room and I get a—"

"No, shit, no. Don't go there." Dominic muttered something in Russian. "I understand."

"You do?" He hopped off the car.

"Yes, I do," Dominic said.

He leaned back on the car. "I found out something tonight. Crista's like … a regular woman. A hot, sexy one."

"Jesus, you've already had sex with her?" Dominic asked.

"No." He rubbed the back of his neck. "I'm saying she's not all about the triathlons. She has dreams about getting married, having kids, and settling down to train others about fitness. There's an uneasiness about her, and for the first time, I don't see another athlete. Bro, she's vulnerable, and I find that sexy. If I strip away my fishing career and her training, we're just a man and woman who kissed."

"What?" Dominic said. "You kissed her?"

He laughed. "I saw her naked as a fish."

"I'm hanging up." Dominic coughed hard. "All I can tell you is to go slow, but fast. To tell her what you want, and don't make her guess. Women get crazy ideas when left alone to think too long. You have to be honest. Endearments help, too, but not 'sweetcheeks'—I called dibs on that one for Diana."

The tension in Bruce's shoulders eased. Dominic's advice was shit, but he understood. Or at least, he was coming around.

"So you think I should go for it?" he asked.

"Oh, boy," Dominic muttered. "I think you know what you want to do. Use your head, not your dick."

He planned to use both. "Thanks, man. I'll let you go."

"No problem. I'll see you in a couple of weeks, yes?" Dominic said.

"What's happening then?" he asked.

"Grayson called and said we're all meeting in Cottage Grove. The women need a Girl's Night Out. He said you were down for coming," Dominic said.

He groaned over forgetting about the plans. "Yeah. I remember. See you then."

He disconnected the call. *Shit.*

Grayson wasted no time. He'd planned the get together to coincide with his two-year anniversary with Shauna. Gary and his wife Angie, Dominic, Diana, Juan, and Dana were all going to be there. He and Crista both cherished the connection with the others. Now they were the only two not married and settled down.

A yearning to belong with Crista, to join their friends as a couple, and to settle down and enjoy life with the one and only person he needed hit him hard. Crista was a part of his life, and he suddenly wanted to scale mountains, see more of the world, hold her in his sleep, and veg on the couch on a Sunday while they teased each other over a bagel.

He wanted it all, and he wanted it with Crista. Not every few months, or daily phone conversations. He wanted to be a part of her daily life, forever.

"That's it," he mumbled, smiling.

He had two weeks to romance Crista and solidify their new relationship. Hell, they were already best friends. They knew more about each other than most married couples do before marriage. They were already better off than Dominic had been when he started seeing Diana, who'd hated Dominic at the start. They got married only a few months later.

There really wasn't anything stopping Bruce from committing himself to Crista.

He marched to the stairwell, entered the apartment building, and kept on going straight up to Crista's apartment. Outside Janelle's apartment, he paused and looked over at the door. He was an idiot. He was also cruel. Crista deserved a man who knew what he wanted, and he never should have asked her to set him up with Janelle.

He continued down the hallway. First thing tomorrow, he'd call the florist and make reservations at an expensive restaurant with a corner table where he could talk to her in private. She needed to know how much he loved her and wanted to have sex with her. No, he couldn't romance her that way. She wasn't the type of woman to jump right into bed. He ran his hands over his face. But she had offered him sex; it was sort of the same thing.

Nah, she wanted a normal relationship. He'd go slow. The wait would be worth it if she was happy. He punched in the code for the apartment and stepped inside, closing the door softly. Without making a sound, he walked through the dark into the living room.

Sex was the only thing they needed to try out to know if they were compatible in all areas, and he had all the confidence in the world after the kiss they'd shared that sleeping with her would rock his world.

The light came on. He whirled around, and everything he'd planned fell apart. Crista stood in front of him naked, vulnerable, and more beautiful than ever. He couldn't move or speak. His heart beat erratically. He gasped for air worse than a fish out of water. Either he was dying or he'd caught the biggest bass of his life.

Chapter Eleven

Crista stood perfectly still at the entrance of the living room. A chill from her nervousness collided with the warmth from inside her body at seeing Bruce. The urge to bring her arms up and cover her naked body stayed in her head. Her body screamed with joy at the intent look coming from Bruce, and her decision to try again with him became stronger.

She'd tossed and turned for the last two hours, debating on whether to wake Bruce or save her confession for the morning when she was thinking straight. But she knew she'd chicken out if she didn't go for it now. She'd never expected him to walk through the door after coming back from Janelle's apartment. From having sex with the bitch. From satisfying himself while she lay wrestling with the biggest decision of her life.

His mouth softened and his eyes locked on hers. She rocked back on her foot, ready to bolt.

"Crista," he mumbled, stepping toward her.

She raised her hand. "Don't."

His brows lowered and he stopped. "What's wr—?"

"I can't do this," she whispered, finally crossing her arms over her naked breasts. "I made a mistake."

"No, you didn't." Bruce nodded. "We can do this."

She shook her head. He had no idea. "N—"

"Yes," he whispered, and she was surprised when his words came out raw and pained. "You can because I heard you say you wanted me."

"I changed my mind." She inhaled swiftly, surprised that he'd heard her. "Don't do this to us. Please. We're friends, this will only come between us, and more than anything, I'm not willing to throw away years of depending on you to always be there for me. I need you more than a stupid mistake."

"We're not a stupid mistake." He stood in front of her, holding her, pressing his large hands against her bare back before she could open her mouth. "It'll only get better."

He kissed her.

Shocked and humiliated, she could only sag against him, taking and believing him. She could no longer voice her opinion or formulate a thought. Her body liked what he was doing, and she trusted him. Stripped of all her defenses about why they shouldn't be standing in the living room—her naked, him dressed—kissing, she did the only thing she could manage to do.

She kissed him back.

Whether it was trepidation, familiarity, plain old forbidden lust, or a mix of all three, she quivered in response. His accustomed rugged scent combined with the warmth of his mouth, created an intoxicating aphrodisiac. Her leg came up with no help from her and wrapped around the roughness of his jeans.

Then Bruce lifted her off her feet. She sank her fingers into his hair without letting go of his mouth. A mouth so foreign and perfect to her, she couldn't get enough.

His lips urged her to open to him. Her heart raced, sending a tremor down her spine and settling in her lower back. She arched her pelvis, hooking her ankles behind his back as she deepened the kiss.

The rocking caress of his body rubbing against hers was her only hint that he carried her out of the room. She stroked his tongue, holding his head in place. The need to have more of him, to explore every inch of his body—a body that until recently, she'd taken for granted because it was his mind and heart that she loved—rolled through her.

Her world tilted. She gasped and landed on the bed, staring at Bruce. She blinked, suspended in time, unable to understand how crazy wild it was that she was flat on her back, naked in front of her best friend. Bruce settled between her legs, and the weight of him atop her body felt better than winning any race.

"I'm going to sink myself inside of you," he whispered.

She nodded; a quiver rolled across her front at his promise and her nipples peaked. "I want that."

The corner of his mouth tightened, and she formed her hand against his jaw. Thrumming his cheek, she knew she had everything right here with her. Her best friend was going to be her lover.

"Condom?"

She stilled. "A condom?"

"Yeah, sweetheart. I need to protect you," he said.

Shit. She turned her head and scanned the room. Where was the last place she had sex? Had she ever bought condoms? Why couldn't she think?

"Uh." She wrinkled her nose. "That might be a problem."

Bruce kissed her neck, bringing her back to facing him, and said, "Stay here."

She opened her mouth to ask him where she'd go with him on top of her, and his body left her. She stared at his back as he left the room. The second he was out of sight, she sat up and hugged her pillow.

How embarrassing. Who knew what Bruce was thinking. He'd come from Janelle's apartment, and no doubt that bitch was a talented, skilled, and a professional lover. *She'd* have condoms. God, they were probably monogramed with her initials on them.

Crista hung her head and closed her eyes. All she did was babble. Next shopping trip, she'd buy all the condoms and keep them next to the bed. Maybe even buy a crystal bowl and display them all as if they were pieces of candy she frequently partook in. She groaned and opened her eyes. If Bruce gave her a second chance, which he probably wouldn't, seeing as how she couldn't compare to Janelle, he'd never catch her unprepared again.

"Hey," Bruce said, approaching the bed. "You okay?"

She frowned. "Truthfully?"

He sat down on the edge of the bed and pulled her over beside him, wrapping his arm around her. "We've always been tight with each other. Nothing about that has changed."

"Okay." She laid her head on his chest, so he couldn't look at her face. "You just came back from screwing Janelle, and that's freaking me out a bit. I don't have any condoms because unlike you, I'm not a whore. I mean, I've slept with guys but it's not something I do in my own house, and you know my track record, I don't do boyfriends because of training. I feel stupid—"

"Shut up," he whispered. "First off, I didn't sleep with Janelle."

She lifted her head off Bruce and studied him. "You didn't?"

He shook his head. "I went outside to the parking garage to call Dominic and I didn't want you overhearing my conversation."

"Why?" She sat up straighter.

"Because I heard every word you said earlier when you thought I was sleeping." He inhaled sharply. "I wanted to tell someone."

She slapped his chest. "Did not!"

"Yeah." He brought her back around to his lap. "I've been thinking a lot."

Oh, God. He'd changed his mind. She pinched the base of her neck. "About?"

"Sex. With you." He hooked her neck and pulled her back. "Every thirty seconds like clockwork."

"But Janelle … "

"There's no Janelle. There never was, and never will be," he said. "There's just you. Right here in bed, nice and warm. My best friend, who I want to fuck."

"Vulgar," she whispered, panting hard.

He grinned. "I'll show you vulgar … and dirty … and—"

"Shut up and do it." She kissed him hard.

After she'd thoroughly kissed him, he stood up and undressed. She sat on the edge of the bed, enjoying the moment, filled with the wonderful feeling that he wanted her, that what they were doing was the right direction for them to go.

He dropped his shirt on her floor. She swallowed past the lump of emotions pressing down on her. He was gorgeous.

Broad, tanned shoulders filled her vision. His chest flexed, and the muscles tightened. She inhaled swiftly as lust, pure and simple female appreciation, coursed through her body. His roughened hands went to his belt. She leaned forward, her nails digging into the comforter on her bed. Eager to see him completely for the first time.

Bruce pushed his jeans off his hips and had them lying on the floor without pausing. She stared, enthralled at his hard cock. She had no idea why knowing Bruce went commando under his jeans impressed her, but it was hot.

He opened his hand. She smiled at the sight of the foil-packaged condom, and held out her arm to take the protection. She slid off the bed and kneeled in front of him. While tearing open the wrapper, she leaned forward and kissed his bare hip, and then the other, purposely avoiding the one part of him she wanted to touch.

Bruce's fingers tangled in her hair and pulled her head back. She gazed up into his face.

"You on your knees in front of me will make this a short night, sweetheart," he said.

She rolled on the condom, taking her time. The heat coming off him excited her. Unable to deny herself, she slowly wrapped her fingers around his hardness. His pelvis thrust forward and he elicited a soft groan. She loved the way he responded, and she grew confident that it was her that he was enjoying.

He slipped his hands under her arms and picked her up, backing her to the bed until her legs hit the mattress, and she sprawled on the top. He put his knee to the mattress. "My turn."

He settled between her legs, his mouth on her sex. Her legs tensed, and then went to liquid. Unable to move, breathe, or think, she felt.

She felt everything.

Every lick, suck, nibble controlled her body. Powerless and prized, she gave herself to him. Her neck arched. She squirmed underneath him, but his hands on her hips settled her down. Warmth spread throughout her limbs. She reached down between her legs and threaded her fingers through Bruce's hair, needing that connection, that proof that this was really happening.

Bruce growled against her. The vibration from the noise sent her hips off the bed. He palmed her ass, not letting her get away. Caught in his hold, she orgasmed hard, fast, and mind-blowingly wonderful.

To her surprise, Bruce continued to caress her with his tongue, letting her enjoy the after jolts continuing to ping her body in the most delightful way. She inhaled deeply and sighed. She smiled because even to her own ears, that was a soft, delicate moan. She'd never once mewed with a man.

But along with bliss came guilt. She closed her eyes and turned her head to the side. Her best friend was between her legs and—

His weight shifted and the warmth of his mouth trailed up her body, over her stomach, settling on her breast, and then on the other breast. Emotional overload and fear consumed her. What if the next time he looked at her, he'd see her as just another woman in the long line of lovers he'd had?

A tear rolled through her lashes, over her temple, and into her hair. She couldn't lose him. Who would she confide in? Who would support her career? She rubbed her eyes and inhaled a shuddering breath. Who'd stay up all night with her, talking about bait and the circumference of a bass's mouth?

"Sweetheart," Bruce said, cupping her face with his hand. "Hey, are you crying?"

She opened her eyes. Concern and confusion met her gaze. "I'm okay," she whispered, hating the way her voice broke.

He was used to confident women who went from one orgasm to the next without messing their makeup or breaking a sweat. She lay underneath him, damp from the ride he'd taken her on, and an emotional basket case.

"Liar," he whispered. "Talk to me."

"We're best friends," she said, hoping that explained everything.

Bruce's mouth softened and his gaze never left hers. He stayed silent for a few seconds, watching her intently, and then he said, "It's more than sex. It's only you I need to be inside of to feel like I belong. No one—" he held her face tighter "—I mean, no one, makes my heart come alive like you do, whether I'm right here between your legs wanting to have sex with you or hearing your voice on the phone because we're in different parts of the world. It's you and me. That's never going to change."

"Seriously?" She held on to his arms, holding him against her.

"Yeah." Bruce glanced down between their bodies. "Promise you."

She ran over his confession in her mind, so she'd never forget. "Do you think we could, uh, since you haven't and I did, maybe you'd like to—"

"Finish?" He stilled above her and the hard length of his cock throbbed against the inside of her thigh. "You can't stop me, sweetheart."

He lowered his head and nuzzled her neck as he slid into her wetness. She trembled at the invasion, the pressure, the size of him. "Oh, boy … " she whispered into his hair.

His pelvis pressed into her and her whole body sang. She wrapped her arms around his neck, holding on to him to keep from careening into another orgasm.

She'd had no idea sex could be this way. She was used to one time and she was done. It was over; there was no going on. Her pussy pulsed, squeezing Bruce's cock, as if proving her wrong. There was more pleasure to come, and she wasn't one to argue with Bruce when she was feeling this good, this happy, this excited.

Bruce pushed up on his hands, hovering atop her, staring down into her face. She stroked his jaw, loving the way he was holding on for her.

His shoulder muscles bunched, and he thrust inside her. Hooded eyes gazed down at her. She arched her pelvis, locking her ankles behind his thighs. Direct pressure hit her in the exact spot she needed every time he plunged in more deeply. Frantic and needy, she undulated her hips trying to catch every caress, every nudge, every stroke.

"Oh, God … " She clasped her hands on his biceps, digging her nails into the hard muscles of his arms.

Bruce panted, moving faster, harder, more deliberately. "That's it, sweetheart."

She moved and reached. Reached and moved. Her core tightened and straightened, heating and coiling hotter with each stroke, each rub, each touch.

"Give it to me," he said, grunting every time he sank balls deep inside of her. "So fucking beautiful."

Bam.

As if he controlled her body, she let go. Every cell fluttered in response. She blinked to keep her eyes open through the overload of pleasure flooding her body from the inside out.

Bruce grunted, thrusting and holding himself stiff. His arms quivered in her grasp, and through his own pleasure, he never once took his gaze off her. Even then, he kept his attention centered on her, for her, giving her everything.

Chapter Twelve

Crista overslept. Bruce remained on his back, his arm around her, and enjoyed the way she'd wound her body around his when she finally gave up the fight and fell asleep. He'd lain wide-awake for the last two hours, selfishly taking the quiet to enjoy a woman's warm body on him.

He stared at the ceiling. No, not any woman … Crista.

Because he'd slept with her, questions plagued him. He needed to call his manager.

Beyond what he was doing in two weeks, he had no idea how to fit Crista into his life. He sure in the hell wasn't going to be satisfied with every other month visits and short phone calls while he traveled the world. She had a job and training to do, so it wasn't like she could fly around with him while he worked.

Crista sighed in her sleep, stretched her leg, and when she was done, pulled her leg up higher until the inside of her thigh settled on his dick. The warmth and pressure was enough to set him off, and he hardened. Aware of the softness of her breasts snuggled against his ribs, he forced himself to act.

"Crista," he said, sliding out from beside her. "Wake up, sweetheart."

He gathered his jeans off the floor and slipped them on. Glancing at the Crista in the bed, his cock throbbed in need, but he only had a short time to fix everything so they could both get to the place where they'd have forever together.

Damn, he'd had no idea how perfect she was with her clothes off. Her breasts, firm and bigger than he'd imagined, overflowed his hands. Her legs—which he'd admired often for their strength and muscle formation, had wrapped around him last night in such a way that he could still feel their imprint on his hips.

Crista rolled to her side and lifted her head. "Bruce?"

Against his better judgment, he approached the bed, leaned down, and kissed her. His blood pulsed. He needed more.

He nudged her mouth open and tasted her tongue. His hand went to the back of her neck, and held her there as he deepened the kiss. Hell with it, he could stay in bed all day and call his manager tonight.

The mattress cushioned his knee. He leaned over her, guiding her back on the bed. His balls tightened, knowing in a few minutes he'd settle himself between her legs and enjoy her again.

Crista planted both of her hands on his chest and pushed. He continued his path down, and ended up belly down on the mattress with Crista nowhere in sight. He turned his head and found her standing beside the bed, arms crossed over her breasts, and her eyes as wide as a reflective bass lure.

"I missed work." She darted her gaze around the room. "Totally missed my class. It's over."

He pushed himself off the bed and stood. "We were up most of the night. You needed your sleep."

A strangling noise came from her and she blinked up at him without saying a word. He straightened his shoulders. She had something to say; he only had to wait for it.

She found her voice. "You let me sleep in?"

"Yeah." He rubbed his hand over his jaw and studied the red marks at the side of Crista's neck. "Shit. I need to shave."

"Are you insane?" She hurried out of the room. "No, don't answer that. This is whacked."

A door slammed and the shower came on. He let his head fall back on his shoulders and gazed at the ceiling. *Women.*

He'd never understand how they could go from hot to cold while he stood there alone with a morning hard-on that needed attention. Maybe he was better off not knowing what went through a woman's head. He walked out to the living room, shucked his jeans, and put on clean clothes. When he finished lacing up his boots, Crista still hadn't come out of the bathroom.

He poured two glasses of orange juice and found a few of the granola bars she kept for mornings when she was in a hurry. He sat one down by her glass, and inhaled two of them himself. Not even food was taking his mind off Crista naked in the shower without him. He wandered back into the living room and sat on the couch. For all he knew, she was in there soaping up her body, rubbing the suds around her breasts, down her stomach, and he was missing out on the opportunity.

He stood and stepped over the coffee table to join her in the bathroom when his cell phone rang. He leaped back over to the couch and swiped the keypad. "Yeah?"

"Coldwell, your tickets will be at the gate and I'll have your itinerary in your hotel room along with your bags," his manager, Dwayne Hagstone, said.

"What day am I flying out?" He plopped down on the couch.

"On Thursday. Three days," Dwayne said.

"What?" He leaned forward and braced his elbow on his knee. "I have another week off."

"Not any longer. Fish and Game contacted the judges last night. The water temperature fell on Lake Konaco. They want the tournament over to restock the lake before they miss their window to replant. We're having to jump through hoops or we'll have to reschedule, which will mess up the world tournament."

"Fine." He rubbed the back of his neck. "Do me a favor and order another plane ticket and upgrade my room to a suite. I'm bringing someone with me."

Dwayne cleared his throat. "Bruce … "

"Don't worry, it's someone special this time," he said.

Dwayne laughed. "Don't bullshit me, Coldwell. Every woman is special for the day. I don't want your head wrapped around another model and not on fishing."

His shoulders tensed. Crista was not just another distraction. "Things have changed since we've talked, and I need to change a few things. All future events will have to be planned for two people. I only want the best hotels, the best service, and while I'm competing, you will see after Crista's safety."

"Crista? That chick that hangs out—"

"Respect, Dwayne. If you want to continue managing my career, then you'll do what I ask. Her name is Crista; use it," he said.

"I hope you know what you're doing," Dwayne said.

"There's no doubt. I'll be there, and I'll take home the win," he said. "I'll call you before we board the plane."

He disconnected the call. Feeling a whole lot better, he set the phone on the couch and went to join Crista in the shower.

The bathroom door opened before he could step inside. He ogled Crista, who somehow had showered and dressed in a pair of biking shorts and a sports bra. He smiled because he knew exactly what would happen when he peeled back the spandex of her bra and let those babies free.

"I can't believe you let me oversleep." Crista pushed past him and continued on to the living room.

He tilted his head to the side and followed the sway of her hips. His fingers itched to cup her ass and haul her over his shoulder.

"You know how important it is to train, and my clients rely on me. How can I expect them to dedicate their lives to being the best, to remaining in top condition, and exercising every single day if I can't even manage to show up for our scheduled training sessions?" Crista lifted one leg and slipped on a low-cut sock then repeated the movement with her other leg. "Not to mention, I need to train. Missing one day will set me back a week. I'm old, Bruce. I can't take time off or everything I worked for will deteriorate into fat and make me weak."

He frowned. He had no idea what she was talking about and decided he'd like nothing more than to kiss the back of her knees. He stepped toward her and leaned over, grabbing her around the thighs.

"What are you doing?" She shrieked when her feet left the floor.

"Bed." He pivoted.

Crista came alive, kicking and tearing at his shirt. "Let me go."

He continued walking, enjoying the feel of her body undulating against him. Her ass, on his shoulder, was a tempting sight. He entered the bedroom and dove on the bed with her, crawling up her body and pinning her wrists to the mattress.

"I need—"

"To shut up." He grinned, taking her mouth with his, and kissing her into submission.

Her movements stopped. Her body softened, and her legs widened, letting him ride the waves of her body as she settled down. He tasted, teased, and set about fully dominating her. It was like reeling in the biggest catch, and she was the trophy.

He loved her for her big attitude, but he enjoyed the competition of making her his. When he got inside her head and touched her body, she melted and he was hooked.

He kissed her softly, easing back little by little, until he was inches from her mouth. "Change of plans, sweetheart. You're flying out with me in three days, so re-arrange your schedule."

She stared up at him. Her dilated pupils mirrored his reflection.

"Then from Washington, we'll fly to Cottage Grove and get together with the others," he said.

Her gaze narrowed. "Washington s—"

"State." He trailed his hand down her hip, pulling her leg tighter against him. "You smell good."

Her hands came off the mattress and she tugged on his shirt. "I can't go."

"Why not?" He shifted, letting her pull the material off his body. "You can train while we travel. You've done it before."

Her fingers sprawled on his chest, kneading his muscles. "Clients." She wiggled underneath him, reaching down for the button of his jeans. "Can't lose my job or I lose my apartment, too."

"Move in with me," he mumbled against her neck as he slid his hand between her shorts and her stomach.

"I can't." She moaned when his finger skimmed over the nub between her legs.

She cried out, a rasping whimper in the room. He quickly yanked her shorts off, using his bare foot to kick them off her feet so he could unfasten his own jeans. Crista's hands continued touching him all over: his chest, his nipples, his stomach.

By the time his cock came from his jeans, he groaned in pleasure. He stretched over her, reaching for a condom on the nightstand. Crista slid down in bed and a hot, moist suction latched onto him. His toes curled and he stared down at his dick in Crista's mouth.

Crista angled her head and gazed up into his eyes, and damned if that wasn't the hottest thing he'd ever seen. His thought process petered out at the stroke of her tongue. It was all he could do to hold himself up on his arms.

She licked in slow, lazy, strokes, then a deep plunge, sending shockwaves through his body. He fisted the blanket, scared of moving in case she stopped.

Her lips tightened and her cheeks indented until dimples appeared on both sides. His pulse, already throbbing, sped faster.

Crista's eyelids fluttered. Warmth flashed over the surface of his skin, knowing she was turned on by taking him with her mouth. His heartbeat centered along the base of his cock, and he wanted inside of her. He wanted to feel her come. He wanted her hard and fast.

"Need you." He growled, hefting his weight to one arm and taking her hand. "On your knees, sweetheart."

Crista scrambled out from under him, rolled over coming up on her knees, and held on to the headboard, presenting her backside to him without any questions or hesitation. He settled between her feet, running his hands over her hips, taking in the rounded shape.

She thrust out her ass, lowering her head, letting her wet hair fall between her arms. He moved in closer, hand on his cock, and entered her pussy slowly. He panted for control, but she all but sucked him in. The sensation almost killed him with pleasure.

"Honey," she gasped. "Now."

He gripped her hips, ready to give her everything he had. He braced her body for his thrust and then grunted as he slid fully into her wetness. The soft cushion of her ass was his reward. Wet and hot, she rocked back for every forward motion he made, meeting him halfway. Her body trembled under his touch and he held on for all he had, knowing she was going to come hard and fast, and he wanted to be ready.

Crista's hair whipped back and lay sprawled along the middle of her back. The arch in her body let him go deeper, and he took full advantage of her position. Keeping a grip on her hip, he used his other hand to grasp her hair and hold her poised in front of him.

"Yes," she hissed out.

His hips spontaneously jerked at the guttural need coming from Crista. He'd had no idea she had it in her to play rough, and he liked the surprise. He lurched and withdrew until the head of his cock almost exited her body then slammed back into her fully. She spasmed around his length and he saw stars. Fucking stars.

"You like that?" He gave her more, knowing she couldn't lie.

Her moans filled the room and their breathing raised the temperature. He tugged her hair, taking the way she lunged back, almost on her heels, slamming into his pelvis. His balls tightened and he quickened his pace.

"Yes, yes, yes …" Crista's body stiffened and she convulsed in front of him, squeezing his come out of him. He pitched forward, letting go of her hair, her hip, and landing on top of her with his hands spread wide on the bed. He closed his eyes to clear his vision and inhaled deeply, exhaling on a shudder.

"Jesus Christ," he mumbled against her shoulder.

Crista laughed on a sigh and collapsed flat on the bed. "I didn't think you had it in you."

He rolled to the side and pulled her into the crook of his body, wrapping his arm around her waist. "What are you talking about?"

She shrugged. "I pictured you smooth and charming in bed. I never imagined you'd like it rough and fast."

"What about you?" He changed the pitch of his voice. "Yes, Yes, Yes," he mimicked her earlier words.

She rolled onto her back and looked at him. "You're asking the girl who'd rather swim the Pacific Ocean than lounge in a pool. I prefer to run twenty-six miles in one event than jog around the block every morning. My bike doesn't have a basket and a bell on the handlebars, honey. If I'm going to fuck you, I'd rather win the prize after it's over."

He'd found the love of his life.

He kissed her forehead and pulled her tighter, and even though he was exhausted and not quite ready for round two, nothing curbed his happiness. He chuckled against her hair, holding her to his chest. She laughed, and soon he'd lost control again and joined in the amusement. He couldn't wait until they were living together.

Chapter Thirteen

Three giant ropes, twenty-five feet long with a diameter of three inches, weighing approximating fifty pounds waved in motion across the room. Crista stood in between the ropes and clapped her hands. "Good job, guys. Next."

Her next three clients moved forward, picked up the end of the rope, and began the up and down motion to get the ropes undulating against the floor. Crista glanced over at Bruce. God, he was sexy.

He talked on his phone quietly, not disturbing her class, but she was aware of him. Full of energy, she put her feet together and jumped over the ropes, grinning at Bob Lackey, who was struggling to keep momentum. She enjoyed her classes, and the extra time to work out meant faster progress for her, too.

"Ten more," she called out, continuing down the line, jumping as if the gym workout was a playground routine instead of some serious exercise. "Five, four, three, two, and done."

The ropes fell to the floor. Bob stumbled back and leaned against the wall. She walked over and planted her hand on his chest, making him stand up straight.

"Inhale through your nose, out through your mouth." She dropped her arm. "Take your pulse."

She paced in front of the room. When ten seconds passed, she said, "Record."

Bob said, "One hundred-two."

"Better. You've improved, Bob. By next week, it'll be down in the double digits. Good job." Crista gazed at Linda and raised her brows.

"Ninety-five." Linda accepted Bob's high five.

"Excellent." Crista moved on down the line, adding four more motivating replies.

After four months, they were all at different levels, but the core group worked well together. Where one person lacked motivation, the others provided the boost. She handed out towels.

"Now you've got two days off. Follow your set program on your own. Remember, I will be able to tell if you slacked off and so will your records … the heart doesn't lie. This isn't about me, it's about you. The only way you'll succeed is to keep pushing yourself. It's much easier to look back and be proud of how far you've come than it is to regret the time you lost." She smiled. "Class dismissed. See you on Monday."

She moved away, heading toward Bruce, when Bob stopped her. She touched his arm. "Yes?"

"I want to thank you." Bob pulled his T-shirt from his chest and fanned the material. "In nine months, I've lost fifty pounds, and while most of the people in our group are training for marathons, I needed to do this for my daughter."

Crista tilted her head. "Your daughter?"

Bob nodded and his smile grew. "I was headed to an early grave, fighting obesity and a long line of ancestors who struggled with Type 2 diabetes. We had our daughter later in life, and I want to watch her grow up, walk her down the aisle, you know … "

Crista nodded. "I understand, and you should be proud of yourself. What has got you this far in your journey is determination?"

"And stubbornness," Bob added, chuckling.

"That always helps, too." Crista laughed.

"Anyways, I wanted to say thank you and let you know I signed up for a 5k. I know it's nothing like a marathon and I can walk or run. It's just a community fundraiser to clean up the beach, but I'm going to finish the race. That's my goal."

"That's excellent." Crista hugged him, slapping him on the back before letting go. "There is no race that's too small. Leave a message on the bulletin board in the office, and I'll make sure I'm there at the finish line to cheer you on, okay?"

Bob grinned. "I'd like that a lot."

Her client walked off to the locker room. She smiled on the way over to Bruce, and now that they were alone in the gym, she wrapped her arms around his waist and waited for him to finish his phone call.

"No, the blue tackle box, and make sure there's extra line in there, too." He ran his hand down her back, finding her bra strap and sliding his finger underneath. "Both the fifty and forty pound weight nylon ones."

She squirmed, tickled from the light touch. It'd been five hours since they'd made love. Touching him intimately, discovering where he liked her hands, her lips, her legs fascinated her. She was discovering another side of Bruce that she hadn't known, and she liked everything she found.

"Okay. Talk to you after I land." He disconnected the call and kissed her upturned lips. "All done?"

"Yep." She moved back. "Thanks for understanding that I had to work today."

"I get it." Bruce picked up her duffel bag. "But now I have twenty-four hours with you all to myself, and I'm not sharing you."

She rolled her eyes. They'd been over her schedule and she'd given him as much of her time as she could allow. "You have four hours with me and then I'm hitting the beach and going for a six mile run. Care to join me?"

Bruce stopped walking. "You're trying to kill me."

"Not at all." She hooked his arm and pulled him out of the gym. "You've got stamina."

"Damn right," he muttered, pushing the elevator button with his free hand. "I'm about ready to prove it as soon as we get up to the room."

She stepped into the empty elevator. "Oh yeah?"

The doors slid shut. Bruce dropped the bag and had her plastered against the side of the elevator before she could stop him. Not that she would've tried.

"Mm … " She nibbled on his lip.

His hands went to her ass and lifted her up until she was straddling his waist. He supported her weight, and she sank her hands into his hair. Her breath caught, and time stopped.

The bell dinged, announcing their arrival to her apartment floor. She groaned and kissed him quickly, before wiggling off him. She was insatiable when it came to him.

"Cruel, honey," she whispered. "Who's the one teasing now?"

"Smart ass." He swatted her ass. The door slid open, and she pranced in front of him and right into Janelle who stood outside the elevator door. Crista stumbled back. "Oh, God. Sorry. I wasn't watching where I was going."

Janelle used her finger and tapped underneath Crista's chin, forcing her to lift her head. "Head high, shoulders back, and carry yourself with confidence … try to walk with feminine prowess and seduction. Then you won't have these little mishaps that always seem to happen to you."

Fury, hot and all-consuming, raged inside of Crista. She fisted her hand and brought her arm back when Bruce snagged her wrist.

"Let's go, sweetheart. Time's wasting." Bruce hustled her down the hall and into her apartment.

She turned on him behind closed doors. "Why did you stop me?"

"I didn't want you to hurt your wrist." He tossed her bag. "Have you ever punched someone before?"

"No." She wrinkled her nose. "But I wouldn't have cared if it hurt me or not. I can't stand her, and she's only getting worse since you came to stay with me."

"Well, we did play her," he said. "She might be a piranha, but I'm sure even they have feelings."

Crista gawked at him. "Are you defending her?"

"No." He reached for her and she slapped his hand away. "I'm just saying it's best if you stay away from her, sweetheart."

She glared. "Fine. Then you go punch her for me."

"Right." He laughed. "I've always had a rule that I don't put my hands on any woman."

She snorted, turned around, and over her shoulder said, "Good rule. From now on, that goes for me, too. Hands off, Coldwell."

"What?"

"You heard me," she yelled from her bedroom.

She stripped out of her clothes and headed to the shower. Women like Janelle were bitter, conniving bitches. She turned on the hot water. Worst of all, Bruce had to witness her humiliation. Nothing like having the woman he'd desired point out everything Crista was lacking. She was not a supermodel and never would be. Nobody had to shove it in her face.

Chapter Fourteen

Bruce scratched his head and gazed down the hall where Crista disappeared in a huff, unsure whether to follow her or give her a few minutes to calm down. Women had mystified him growing up, and they continued to baffle him as an adult. Especially Crista because she'd always seemed to be above the petty sniping women threw at each other.

She never acted upset when Shauna or Diana teased her. Hell, even Angie and Dana fell right into being friends with Crista as if they'd known each other for years. But something about Janelle rubbed Crista the wrong way. They were too different to have ever been real friends.

He walked toward the bedroom, paused outside the bathroom when he heard the water running, and continued into the room. He fell onto the top of the bed and rolled to his side, propping his head on his hand. There was only one way to put things back on even ground for Crista.

Heaving himself off the bed, he stripped off his clothes. Then he made the bed, closed the drapes, and tossed a condom on the pillow. He hesitated for a second and threw a second condom on the bed, too. Exercise always made Crista hot, and just seeing and touching her got him hard as a rock.

The bathroom door clicked open. He turned around and strode to the door, so when she entered the room, he was right there. She glanced down at his cock and reached out to the doorframe to steady herself.

He flexed his chest and grinned. Oh yeah, he still had it.

"That's unfair." She unknotted the towel between her breasts and let it slip to the floor.

"All's fair in love and war, sweetheart." He scooped her up and carried her to the bed.

He laid her down unrushed because he wasn't insensitive. Whatever Crista was upset with Janelle about, he planned to rectify her worries. He slowly turned her to face him.

"There's something special about the times when it's just us." He linked his hand with hers, and lay face to face. Her leg draped over his, he felt more comfortable than he'd ever been with any other woman. "I like this."

"You do?" She placed her head on his arm.

He kissed her forehead. "Yeah."

"Me too." She sighed. "You're warm."

"You're chilled." He untangled his fingers and rubbed his hand down her bare arm. "Soft. So damn soft."

"Cocoa butter," she mumbled.

That was the scent that he could faintly smell. He inhaled, wanting to absorb the soft, light fragrance. "It's good."

"Better than Janelle's scent?" She lifted her head.

He studied her, and only found curiosity. "Y… es."

She laid her head down. He was getting nowhere with her. She kept everything bottled inside under a tough exterior. It was almost as if she was jealous of Janelle.

"Stop thinking about Janelle," he said.

She shifted her leg and shrugged. "Kind of hard not to when she's determined to put me down in front of you every time we run into her, and it sure seems as if that happens a couple times a day."

He sprawled his hand on her hip and pulled her closer until her breasts pressed against his chest and her sex cradled his thigh. He growled at the warmth permeating his skin and ducked his head to nibble on her neck. "Forget about Janelle."

"Hm … " Crista caressed his shoulder. "Make me."

Never one to back down, he rolled until he was settled between her legs and took her nipple in his mouth. Sucking on the hardened bud, he rubbed his length against her sex lightly. Crista's swift inhale sent his heart hammering in his chest. A quiet but fierce need to calm her soul and make everything right in her world settled into passion.

Crista grabbed his hair, dragging him up. He stared down into eyes that shone with her arousal. "Janelle who?"

He grinned and dove for her neck. A skim of his tongue, a nibble from his lips, and he found the heat coming off the curve of her body where her collarbone protruded. He latched onto her skin, sucking gently, wanting to mark her. The act was juvenile and egotistical, but she was his and he wanted everyone to know.

Crista's hand went between their bodies. He sucked in his breath and his toes curled at the firm grip on him. Her fingers worked their magic until his balls tightened and he grabbed her wrist, dragging her arm above her head.

Her gaze nearly stole his breath in its intensity. Without letting her go, he used his other hand to touch her. The softness of her skin, the fragileness of her petite size compared to his was a map of a land he wanted to discover. His fingers slid over her flat stomach, her pubic bone, and between her legs. He shuddered in pleasure as the heat and wetness coated his finger.

In tiny circles, he paid attention to the nub peeking out between her folds, begging for his touch. He opened his mouth to inhale more air. The room grew hotter, and his muscles were hard and demanding, working to stay in control.

Crista's breath caught. He shifted his pelvis and placed his cock at the entrance to her sex. Bracing himself with both arms, he held himself still.

"Tell me what you want." His hips moved and he teased her with his length.

"You," she whispered, lowering her arms and raking her fingernails along his ribs, down his sides. "Forever."

He smiled and gave her an inch. Her legs spread apart more, giving him access. Every cell in his body screamed to plunge inside of her and take everything she was offering. But he held back.

He wanted to enjoy every second, make it last forever, and give her everything she wanted. "What do you need?"

"You." There was no hesitation. Her hands pulled on his biceps, trying to push herself onto him more. "I need you—" she panted "—inside me."

One more shift of his hips and he was farther inside of her. He closed his eyes an extra beat, luxuriating in the pulse of her muscles squeezing, kneading, caressing him. It was almost too much.

"Who loves you?" he whispered, shocked to hear the *thrumb* in the base of his throat of his heart pounding.

She slid her hands around his neck, pulling herself off the bed, and kissed his mouth. A soft, gentle kiss that carved her name on his soul. When she pulled away with small kisses, easing herself down until she looked up into his eyes, she said, "You do."

"Damn right," he muttered, plunging into her balls deep.

Crista's eyes fluttered and she gasped. The scene before him was an erotic dream. He plunged into her and rolled, taking her with him, until she straddled his body and sat on top. His hands went to her hips, holding her there.

"Show me how much you love me, sweetheart." He lifted her up an inch to get her going.

She planted her hands on his chest and lifted her ass, until the head of his cock was the only thing remaining inside her body. She sucked in her lower lip debra caught it between her teeth. Her whole body trembled and he had a hell of a time not putting his hands on her to impale her back on him.

"Do you want me?" she said, her voice no more than a whisper.

"Fuck, yeah," he said.

He held his breath, waiting for more of her heat to encase him. In the slowest, most painful pleasure possible, she lowered herself on him. His fingers tightened on her thighs, holding her in place.

She moistened her lips. "Do you need me?"

He nodded, unable to find his voice and having to clear his throat. "Absolutely."

Her nails dug into his skin. His legs stiffened and the blood pounded in his lower half, numbing him to anything but what she was doing to him.

"I don't … need to ask anymore." She plunged all the way down and leaned forward. With her lips upon his mouth, she whispered, "I love you."

He growled, unable to take anymore, and captured her lips. His hands went to her ass and guided her movements. So slick, hot, and tight she fucked him.

Crista cried out, a whimper of pleasure, and went limp atop him. He rolled her over and thrust once, twice, three times, and held himself deep inside her as he climaxed. Light exploded behind his eyes as his body rocked against her, one jolt after another. And then, before the world stopped spinning and the shockwaves wore off, he kissed her with everything he was feeling.

Several minutes passed, and he finally found the strength to shift his weight onto one arm and roll to the side. His fingers tangled in her hair, now dry from her shower. He took in her beauty, her contentment, and he swore if he had to kill himself making love to her every hour of every day, he would die a happy man.

Chapter Fifteen

Two days later, Crista stood in front of the open doorway of her apartment. She hefted her bicycle onto her shoulder and faced Bruce. He wanted to talk, and she needed to train.

"So, you're going to move in with me?" he asked.

"I gave you forty-eight hours, and have only taken minimal time to exercise, just so we could spend more time together. Why didn't you ask me that question before I'm heading out the door?" She leaned forward and kissed his lips. "Later, okay?"

"Later, we'll be having sex." He put his shoulder to the door and crossed his arms. "Let me hire someone to come and pack up your apartment. You can take care of your clients and rearrange for someone else to take over your job in the fitness complex. The plane leaves tonight, so we're running out of time."

She swallowed. He'd asked her three times in the last two days to move in with him, and until now she'd been able to distract him without giving him a straight answer. She wasn't ready to make a life changing decision when the Ironman was coming up in a few months. She had to find another job, and she had clients that depended on her. There were too many people relying on her, and though she knew this would be her last Ironman, she had no idea what she was going to do afterward or where she could get hired to do what she loved.

"We already made plans to live together, but I need time. I have a lot to do and a lease … " she said. "Please. We'll talk later."

"We leave tonight." He raised his brows. "I can't leave you here."

"Why not?"

His jaw hardened and he glanced down at the floor. "I need you, sweetheart."

His confession wrapped around her heart and penetrated her doubts. She shifted the bike, which was digging into her shoulder. "After I put in a few hours training today and clear my head, I'll discuss how we'll move in together. Right now ... I can't think past what you did an hour ago."

His gaze snapped to hers, and his lips softened. She smiled at him. He'd challenged her by saying he'd never had sex with a woman who was standing on her head. She'd proven to him and herself it was totally possible when the woman is strong enough to hold herself up by her arms and a lot shorter than the man. She kissed him quickly. "I'll see you later."

She escaped before she could change her mind and tell him she wanted to move in with him more than she wanted to compete. To do that would be admitting defeat. She was worn out and tired of the constant training. It also made her doubt everything she thought she believed in. How could she be sure she was doing the right thing by moving forward with Bruce if she changed her mind about a lifelong dream? What if she decided Bruce was a better friend than lover in a few months or a year?

She was not a quitter, but her thoughts were more about ending her career and starting in a new direction. For some reason, she couldn't wrap her head around giving up.

She punched the elevator button harder than necessary. Her head was going to explode if she didn't get out and get in her zone.

"Hey, Crista," Janelle called out.

Crista's shoulders sagged and the bike cut into her muscle. "Hey back."

Janelle strolled down the hallway on five-inch pumps, even though it was only seven o'clock in the morning. Crista took in her cocktail dress, her immaculately made up face, and the waves of hair cascading over her shoulders. No doubt, the woman never needed to sleep.

"I was wondering how you're doing?" Janelle hitched her hip and planted her hand on the bony angle. "I haven't seen you around, and your boyfriend hasn't come out of the apartment in two days."

The elevator doors slid open. She stepped in between them, trying to make her escape without telling Janelle anything about her private life. "We've been busy. I'm late for training. I'll catch up with you later."

She stepped through the doorway and breathed a sigh of relief when the doors closed and Janelle stayed on the other side. Just thinking about Bruce wanting that woman and what they could've done together irritated her. She snorted. Irritated was too mild a word. Janelle plain pissed her off.

Too late now, Bruce was hers, and Janelle was out of the running. *I win.*

Ten minutes later, limber and warmed, she threw her leg over the bicycle seat and stopped. The hair on her nape tickled her.

A Velcro pouch attached to the handlebars was not there the last time she rode, and she never put anything on her bike. Clean lines meant everything to keep the bicycle wind efficient. She opened the flap and pulled out a cell phone.

Before she could decide where the phone came from and what it was doing on her bike, it vibrated in her hand. She looked at the screen and read the incoming text.

It won't ring and bother you on your ride. Call if U have an emergency or need me. Or if you feel like it. Ride safe.

She looked away from the phone and scanned the beach across from the apartments. Satisfied that no one was watching her, she tapped the screen and smiled when a small keyboard popped up. She texted back. *I don't ride with a phone.* Two seconds later, Bruce typed: *You do now. Don't want anything happening 2 U.*

She smiled and held the phone to her chest. Her stomach fluttered and she had the wild urge to laugh. No one had ever taken care of her before. Sure, Bruce in his best friend status had tried, but this was different. It was good.

She typed: *Thanks. I mean that.*

He ended their conversation with a smiley face, so unlike Bruce's rough and gruff exterior, but so like the man she'd gotten to know in bed. She slipped the phone back in the pouch, shaking her head at how mushy she was feeling over carrying it. He always bugged her about going out of the apartment without her cell, and no matter how many times she explained that she had no use for one, he never gave up.

Now because they had sex, he thought he could get away with bullying her. She hopped on the bike and pedaled. She'd give herself one mile to get her head in the route and wipe the contented smile from her face.

Maybe it was okay to be thrilled with the overbearing attention from a man. He supported her and only wanted to protect her. She liked the attention, obviously, going by her happiness. Maybe she could find a way to move with him too … *shit.*

He'd never even mentioned in which one of his houses he wanted them to live together. How could she leave when she had no idea where she was going?

She adjusted her gears and left the boardwalk, heading toward the hill on Seventy-Eighth Street. Later, after her ride, she'd have all her answers, and really, it wasn't so much the what, if, and buts that needed to be settled. She was okay with anything he wanted to do within reason and in a responsible time frame because he meant the world to her.

Her feelings went beyond friendship or sex. He was her soul mate. He understood her needs better than she did, and deep down, she enjoyed having him shouldering some of the things for which she'd always been solely responsible. Maybe that's what she'd been training for her whole life and why lately she'd been feeling unsettled—because she was tired of being single. She wasn't striving for independence or to be the best but to fill her life with someone she loves. She put more power into the pedals and leaned forward on her bike. She liked the thought of being a couple.

For her, it was only him. It'd always been him, even before she realized he was the one she wanted. She'd tested the dating scene before, and everyone she'd met lacked that one thing she desired. Bruce saw past her tough exterior and treated her like the woman she was—the woman she hid from everyone else. A woman he wasn't afraid to stand up to and make feel cherished.

She no longer had a decision to make. Her heartbeat increased and the endorphins kicked in. She wanted to be with him, and she'd be flying out with him tonight. Decision made.

She shifted to a lower gear and stood up on the pedals, putting her leg muscles behind the force getting her up the hill. Her mind cleared and she focused on what was ahead. Left, right. Left, right. Inhale through her nose, exhale out her mouth.

For the next twenty miles, she lost herself in her mental zone. Nothing existed, and it was pure contentment.

A hundred feet from the top of the last and longest five-mile hill, a hiss followed by a drag on her back tire brought her to a stop. She planted her feet on the ground and looked behind at the bicycle. Her inner tube slowly deflated, leaving her rim on the asphalt.

"Shit." She climbed off the bike and carried it over to the grassy area on the side of the road, well away from traffic, and next to the cliff overlooking the Pacific Ocean.

She flipped the lever under her seat and pulled the whole apparatus off. She peered down into the frame tube and frowned. In the chaos of the last few days, she'd spaced on replacing a spare inner tube and pump back in its hidey hole.

A car drove by without stopping. She looked down the hill at how far she'd ridden. Running the twenty-six mile distance back to the apartment would be possible if she didn't have her four thousand dollar bike to carry. The first thing she taught others while training was to protect themselves from injury. She did not need to tweak her shoulder or throw off her pace because she was stupid enough to leave her spare parts at home in the corner of the living room.

Her only course would be to hike to the top of the hill, find the nearest phone, call Mr. Fredrickson, and have him …. She squealed, remembering Bruce's gift of the cell he'd fastened on her bike. "Oh, Bruce. You rock hard, honey."

Delighted over Bruce's thoughtfulness, she quickly retrieved the cell and dialed her home phone. Disaster turned to excitement because now she could go back and spend the day with Bruce and hit the pool after dinner to do extra laps to make up for her failed bike ride.

The phone stopped ringing and a familiar feminine voice said, "Hello?"

Her back stiffened. Had she pushed the wrong button?

"Janelle?" she asked.

"Yes. Hang on a second." Janelle spoke to someone in the background, and Bruce's voice came across the line, answering her.

Crista pulled the phone away from her ear and stared at the screen. No, she'd definitely called her home phone and not Janelle's phone.

"Okay, I'm back. What do you need?" Janelle said.

"Uh … why are you answering my phone?" She pinched the bridge of her nose, not liking the panic rising in her.

"Bruce asked me to." Janelle giggled. "We're busy, so can you call back?"

"Busy?" She grew dizzy, and forced herself to breathe. "It's not even eight o'clock in the morning. What are you doing in my apartment?"

Janelle lowered her voice. "What do you think I'm doing? Bruce asked me over. I really need to, uh, get back to Bruce … so, if you don't need anything, I'm going to hang up."

Dead air filled Crista's ear. Her chest tightened. How could he?

The moment she'd left the apartment, he jumped right back to wanting Janelle, and obviously he'd gotten want he wanted because she was in *her* apartment. Crista gazed down at herself. Sweaty from the ride, she had no makeup on, her old workout clothes were plastered to her body, and her hair was up in a sleek ponytail. Rage built up inside her. Damn Bruce. Damn Janelle.

If he was looking for a supermodel, then he could have the bitch. She clutched the cell in her hand, whirled, and sent the phone flying over the cliff. She wasn't changing for anyone, especially Bruce. She was who she was, sweaty tank and all, and if Bruce couldn't see that, then he deserved to be miserable with Janelle.

Chapter Sixteen

Bruce stood in the middle of the empty living room. He'd had four hours to pack and put everything Crista owned in the moving van, and after recruiting everyone he could find in the apartment complex, they'd accomplished the impossible. All that was left was the equipment Crista used to train, a couple of suitcases Janelle packed for her that'd last for two weeks until they arrived home, and his own luggage he'd brought with him. Even he impressed himself with his rather impromptu organizational skills.

Now all he had to do was tell Crista she was moving now. He rocked back on his heels. If he'd left it up to her to pack, she would've dragged her feet. They didn't have that much time. Besides, he'd accomplished most everything, and now she could relax and not worry.

The door opened and Crista walked in with her bicycle over her shoulder. Proud of himself, he widened his stance and waited for her to notice he'd taken care of everything and she didn't need to lift a finger.

Her brows rose and her mouth opened as she took in her bare apartment. Finally, she dropped the bike with a clattering *thunk*. He stepped toward her, but she put her hand up, stopping him. This was not the reaction he'd imagined receiving.

"Where are my things?" she said.

He tightened his lips over his teeth. For the first time, he wondered if he'd pushed her too fast. He thought women liked surprises, and she'd liked the phone he fastened to her bike earlier. Clearing an apartment out wasn't much different. "About a half hour away, heading north on I-5, in a moving van."

She looked at him, looked at her bare room, and settled her gaze on her bike lying at her feet. Fuck. He was in trouble.

"I know how much you still have to do with your clients; I thought I'd settle things here at your apartment. I already paid the rest of your lease, since you won't be working downstairs in the gym to keep up your end of the agreement. I gave your food to the Fredricksons because they need all the help they can get living on social security, and I knew you'd want to help them," he said, hating the way he sounded desperate. "Now you can concentrate on making your contacts and we'll be ready to go tonight without leaving anything behind to worry about."

She stepped over the bike and walked down the hall without saying a word. He blew out his cheeks and expelled the air while she was gone. She was supposed to be happy. They were starting a new life together. He'd taken care of everything, and all she had to do was concentrate on being happy.

Crista returned to the living room with both his bags hanging from her sides. She approached him and dropped the luggage at his feet.

His chest tightened. "What's wrong?"

"Get out," she whispered.

He stared in disbelief. Her eyes shone bright with emotion and her chin pointed at him in disapproval. He shook his head, trying to understand what he'd done wrong and came back empty. Okay, he'd cleared her apartment out without her asking, or actually giving her consent on moving in with him, but this was Crista. She'd come around and when they were in the air, flying to Washington, she'd be thankful for all his hard work.

"Sweetheart, give me—"

"Get out." She crossed her arms and stepped away from him. "I'm not leaving with *you*, and I'm not moving in with *you*. If our friendship means anything to *you*, give me that much without arguing with me."

"What the fuck is going on?" he mumbled, refusing to move an inch. "I love you."

The words seemed to bounce off her. She closed her eyes an extra beat and when she gazed back at him, she wasn't really looking at him. He reached for her and she trembled, so he dropped his hand. He hated seeing her upset and pushing him away, and he hated not knowing what had happened.

Respecting her, he kept his distance. "You're killing me."

"That's the last thing I'd want to do," she said, her voice hollow and lacking her normal joy for life. "But if you don't leave, you're going to rip my heart out and I don't know if I can survive when that happens. Please. Go. Please."

She frightened him. Something had happened, and he was damn sure her change in attitude had nothing to do with him packing up her apartment. She'd been right there with him this morning in bed, rocking his world, blowing his mind, and loving every second of it.

"Okay." He cleared his throat. "I don't understand what's going on, but I'll give you space."

She remained quiet. He inhaled deeply. "I have an hour before we have to leave for the airport. I'll go down to the beach and come back in thirty min—"

"No." She sniffled. "I'm not going with you, and you're leaving."

The hell he'd leave her alone like this. "I'm calling Shauna, and she's going to talk to the other girls. I'm not going to leave you alone. If you won't talk to me, talk to them, okay?"

She pinched her lips together and nodded.

He stepped toward her one more time, backing her against the wall. She could protest all she wanted, but he was damned if he was going to walk away from her without her knowing how much it hurt him to drop everything.

He hooked her neck and held her in place. Tension warmed his fingertips, and he brought his forehead down on hers. "Don't think I'm running away, sweetheart. You've left me no choice. I have to go to Moses Lake, but I am not giving up on us, on you.

I'll call you tonight, and if you don't want to talk, I'll call you tomorrow morning. I'll keep trying to talk with you until I'm done in Washington and I can get my ass back here to you. I love you, don't you forget that."

She gazed at his feet. He pulled back on her hair, raising her face to his. Her eyes heated, and she shuddered from his touch. She could deny everything, but he saw her respond. He kissed her softly, barely touching her lips with his, and sighed heavily. "Love you, sweetheart."

She dropped her chin to her chest again, and he stepped away, picked up his luggage, and walked away from her. He closed the door softly behind him, and stood in the hallway, beaten.

Without wasting time, he pulled out his cell phone and called Shauna. But the call only added to his frustration and feelings of being useless when he couldn't answer any of her questions.

"I hope to hell Grayson told you what's going on with me and Crista," he said as soon as Shauna said hello.

"Uh, yeah. I knew something was up when we visited California, so I asked him. He talked," she said.

"Then tell me why Crista's making me leave," he said. "She won't listen, and fuck … you should see her. It looks like someone ripped her heart out, and her devastation is aimed at me. I don't know what I did."

"Listen, honey. When a woman won't even be in the same apartment complex with you, something is seriously wrong," Shauna said.

"That's what I've been trying to tell you." He clamped his hand on the back of his neck and rotated his shoulders. "She's scaring me. Crista never lets anything get her down and she's about as low as I've ever seen her. She always talks to me and a few minutes ago, she barely even looked at me. I need you to fly out here and be with her. Someone needs to make sure she's okay."

"Okay. Let me get ahold of Grayson at the tennis center and have him come home and watch the baby. I'll be on the first flight I can get. Meanwhile, I'll talk to the other girls and see if Crista happened to call one of them. I'll keep you posted," Shauna said.

"Thank you. Call me. Whatever you hear or don't, I want to know." He disconnected the phone.

In his head, he knew he was doing the only thing he could manage to do. In his heart, he hurt for Crista. He loved her, and wanted to do more.

He stepped closer to the apartment door and leaned against the wood, straining to hear anything coming from Crista, but the apartment remained quiet. He left the door and walked to the elevator as if he'd never see her again. Nothing was real.

They'd never fought before. They'd bickered, they'd teased, and they'd grown tired of each other's company in the past, but she had never pushed him away. If he weren't due for a tournament, he'd stick around town and keep trying to talk with her. But he had to compete.

His tourneys paid his bills and allowed him to travel the world. Not to mention, he was the reigning world-class bass fisherman of the fucking world, and he wasn't giving that title up any day soon. He exhaled loudly. Hell, he'd give the title up if that meant having her back with him and happy.

The elevator doors opened and Janelle stepped forward and laid her hand flat on his chest. "Oh, Bruce … you aren't leaving already, are you?"

His body turned cold. "Go find someone else to bother, Janelle."

"Bruce … " Her lower lip came out and she leaned against him. "Is that any way to talk to your girlfriend's best friend?"

He slung one of his bags into the elevator and grabbed her wrist before she could do anything else to embarrass herself. "You go near Crista, and you'll find yourself shacking up with your manager and out of an apartment. I don't want you going near Crista or even saying her name. Do you understand me?"

She scoffed. "You can't kick me out of my apartment."

"Try me." He dropped her arm and skirted around her. "Money talks, babe, and I have plenty around to make sure Crista's happy. If that means getting you away from her and out of this apartment complex, I'll do it. Cast your line somewhere else because we're both done with you."

Janelle glared and pursed her lips, creating wrinkles where real skin ended and Botox started. He pushed the lobby button on the panel of the elevator and watched the doors close, blocking out the woman who made Crista upset half the time she came around. He had no idea what had made him think Janelle was a catch. Crista was spot on. Janelle was a barracuda.

He rode the elevator down to the first floor, checked his watch, and headed to his rental car. He had two hours free, and he might as well turn in the vehicle and check in with Shauna again to make sure she was able to get away. One thing he was sure of, he wouldn't get on the plane without knowing someone was taking care of Crista. No matter if he blew the tournament and stayed in Cali. Crista's happiness meant more than money or his career.

Chapter Seventeen

According to her wristband pedometer, Crista had walked four and a quarter miles since Bruce left. She continued to pace the apartment. Her chest ached and despite the small area, now bare of her belongings and what she couldn't deem as real exercise, she panted for breath.

She hurt worse than anything she'd ever experienced.

Her stomach spasmed. Her heart raced. Her head pounded.

Most of all, she was numb and had to keep reminding herself that Bruce had cheated on her. He might not have actually screwed Janelle, but he'd had her in the apartment *keeping her busy*. She sniffed and pivoted on her foot to continue marching down the hallway.

He'd ripped her heart out and left her vulnerable. She pressed her hand to her chest without missing a step. She hated being vulnerable.

She sniffed. *I will not cry.*

Worst case scenario, she'd still see Bruce in social gatherings any time their group of friends got together in Cottage Grove or at an Olympian event. Her friends would expect her. His friends would demand Bruce's appearance. She stumbled and caught herself on the wall. God, how could she see him again knowing what they had, what they could do in bed together, what he meant to her?

She held her breath and squeezed her eyes closed. *I will not cry.*

Bolstering through the pain, she forced herself to keep moving. She sought the place where her mind emptied and her body moved automatically. Only in the athletic zone would she escape the pain of his betrayal and the worst day of her life.

The doorbell rang. She froze. He wouldn't come back and blow any chance of them remaining friends, would he?

"Crista, open the door," a voice sounding exactly like Shauna's penetrated her apartment.

Relief swept through her, leaving her shaky. Bruce had kept his word on calling in the girls to take care of her. She ran to the door, flung it open, and soaked in all the female karma coming from Shauna, Dana, Diana, and—she blinked at Gary's wife Angie. Her vision blurred, and before she could motion them inside, they'd surrounded her. Protected within the safety of her girls, she finally allowed herself to do what she never succumbed to in competition.

She cried.

She'd lost.

She'd failed.

Arms gently guided her inside. With her friends' help, she sat on the floor, bookended by Shauna and Diana on each side of her. She held her face in the palms of her hands and gasped through the sobs. Between wails of self-pity and sorrow, she told them every little detail.

The mixed feelings, the declaration of love, Bruce's fascination with Janelle, her own lack of confidence, and most of all how much finding out Bruce invited Janelle to *her* apartment hurt her. She had no idea how long she talked, but she continued until her eyes were swollen and she'd destroyed a half a box of Kleenex.

When she couldn't cry any more, she leaned against Diana and stared at Dana who sat on the floor across from her. Juan's pretty, kindhearted wife wiped the tears from her own face, making Crista feel even worse. Every one of them came from a different background, but they had one thing in common: their men were all professional athletes just like Bruce.

"I'm sorry." She lifted her head off Diana and swiped her cheeks with the back of her hands. "I don't know why I fell apart. I never do this, and I didn't mean to put all of you in a bad position, being

Bruce's friends, too. I would never have called you … not yet. Bruce should've just left, and forgotten about me."

"That's part of your problem." Diana nudged her with her shoulder. "You're strong and badass. Bruce—God, he's like the rest of our men. He'll treat you like you're incapable of putting a new toilet paper roll on the hanger. It's a jock trait. He's bound to take care of you and if he can't do it, he'll call everyone he knows to fix the problem."

"Great … " She curled her lip. "Now I'm a problem."

"We're not saying that," said Shauna. "It's just that I heard Bruce's voice. He seemed sincere, and he was scared. Our guys don't get scared unless there's a reason to be worried."

"Yeah, he's scared I caught him with the bitch down the hall," Crista muttered. "He pushed and pushed me, and now I've lost all my belongings."

"I love when Juan forces me to let him make the decisions." Dana crawled closer and sprawled out on her stomach near Crista. "Before I met him, you should've seen me. I walked around as if I had a stick up my ass and I was late for the business deal of my life. Because he never gave up or pressured me about my need to organize every little detail, I found out it was okay if I wasn't always in charge. The weird part was, I needed to use him as an excuse to step back and calm down."

Crista drew up her knees and wrapped her arms around her legs. Was that what she was doing? No … she'd already decided to step back from competing and concentrate on training others before he'd shown up. Bruce had fallen into her plans; he hadn't tried to change her.

"There's more to it than personalities clashing or one of us wanting to change." She plopped her chin on her upturned knees. "He coerced me into setting him up with Janelle. We totally baited her. I helped him get close to her. He came to me … okay, I went to him afterward, but we both know he wanted Janelle before me. She's perfect. You all would hate her on sight."

Shauna snorted. "Damn right. Any woman who stabs any one of us girls in the back gets put on our hate-for-life list."

"We have a list?" Diana raised her brows. "Who's on it?"

"Every bitch that Grayson ever dated, dreamed about, talked to, or looked at more than three seconds," Shauna said. "Including the sixty-two-year-old cashier at the store back home. Little slut, always helping him load the cart and taking it to his car for him … and he lets her."

Angie nodded. "Gary's old one night stands are on the list, too. Not the ones who flirted with him and failed. Just the ones he slept with."

"Every woman in the world, except the ones in this room, and especially the woman who gave Juan that stupid nickname. If I knew who she was, I'd punch her in the throat," Dana said.

"Amante Español," Shauna muttered. "Sexy name, but wrong … so wrong."

Even though they were trying to make her feel better, they were all forgetting one important thing. She inhaled and swallowed so hard, they all heard the gulp. "It's different. You all have your man in your life. I don't. Bruce is my best friend … no offense, but he gets me. I lost everything today because I couldn't win over Janelle. I can't see him again because it'll destroy me, and that means I'll never be around when everyone gets together. I just can't. It feels like I'm dying and he's only been gone a few hours."

To her surprise, through the pain, she was also angry, and that antagonism was directed at Janelle. Crista had sat back and watched her so-called friend go after every man in the apartment complex who had a girlfriend or worse, was married. Instead of telling her off for the bitch she was, she'd tried to remain on friendly terms because they were neighbors.

Enough was enough though, and if someone didn't stop Janelle's nasty little habit, the supermodel was going to break up a sacred union. Crista stood, her mind finally made up on how she could solve one of her problems.

"Wait." Shauna heaved herself off the floor and grabbed her arm. "What are you doing?"

"To cross one bitch off the hate-for-life list," she said, walking to the door.

"Oh, shit," Diana said. "She's going to kill the supermodel."

"Stop." Angie ran to the door and blocked Crista from leaving. "Let's talk about this. Maybe there's more to the story and Bruce is innocent. Have you ever thought of that?"

"Innocent? Janelle answered my phone. Bruce was with her, I heard his voice. There's nothing more to say," Crista reached around Angie's slim waist and pulled on the door, forcing her friend to move away. "I'm done feeling sorry for myself and comparing how I look and act to a woman who fried her brain from all the hair dye and diet drugs she's abused for the last five years. She's not ruining my life or anyone else's, ever again."

She marched out of the apartment, down the hall, and knocked on Janelle's door. When Janelle opened it, Crista said, "For three years, I've stood back while you made a fool of yourself by going after everyone's man in the apartment building, but it stops now."

"What are you talking about?" Janelle fluffed her hair. "I'm getting ready for a party, and I don't have time to figure out your simple little problems when I have a big decision to make that involves Armani and Klein."

Defensive and pissed, Crista planted her foot in the doorway, blocking the door from slamming. "What makes you think you're better than I am? That you can flirt and steal Bruce away from me?"

Janelle's perfectly arched brows grew even higher. "Is that what he said?"

"No. In fact, he hasn't mentioned your name … at all." Crista leaned forward and lowered her voice. "Stay away from him. Do not call. Do not try to contact him. Do not even breathe the same air as him."

"He doesn't have a ring on his finger yet," Janelle said, smirking.

Score one for the blonde. Crista poked Janelle in the shoulder. "Back off the men who are already taken, or the next time I'm going to deck you so hard, you'll swallow those shiny white caps on your teeth."

"She'll pop a boob, too." Diana added from behind her.

Janelle gazed over Crista's head at Diana and sneered. "I'm not scared of you little girls, playing your high school days over again in my hallway."

Crista shook her head. "You're pathetic. You can deny your behavior all you want, Janelle, but that's the real reason you relied on my friendship for the past few years. No other woman would put up with the competition. They wouldn't allow you to be a part of their everyday life because you're fake and manipulative. But guess what? None of the men you screwed around with are in your apartment right now, are they? You don't have someone to satisfy you in bed or out of bed because all they see is a desperate woman. You're going to spend your life trying to find the one good man who would give you everything, and you can't even recognize him through your false eyelashes when you see him."

She turned around and slung her arm around Diana's back. "Come on, let's go. I'm done here."

Halfway back to her apartment, Janelle called Crista's name. She glanced at Diana and turned around. "What?"

"You're wrong." Janelle glanced down the other end of the hallway and continued. "I didn't have sex with Bruce while everyone was in the apartment packing your belongings because if I had, you can bet he'd be with me and not you."

Crista stared at the other woman. *Her belongings?*

Her heart raced at the bit of news. She played the day's events back through her head. She went for a ride, got a flat, called Bruce, talked to Janelle, hiked a mile, and called a taxi, and then sat out on the boardwalk for an hour while she calmed down enough to go up and tell Bruce to leave. In the meantime, Janelle said everyone helped Bruce pack her apartment. She'd been gone three, maybe four hours max. There was no way Bruce could manage to clear her apartment out by himself if he was having sex with Janelle instead.

No freaking way.

Adrenaline flooded her body. She grabbed Diana's hand. "I need my phone."

"I'm on it," Diana said, pulling her into the apartment. "Get the girl a phone. She's come to her senses and needs to act fast before her man gets away."

Crista thrust her hands in her hair in frustration and shook her head. "You all knew Bruce didn't sleep with Janelle, didn't you?"

Shauna handed her a phone. "Bruce plays around, but he's not the type to hurt you or throw your friendship away. I had all the confidence in the world that when he called me to check on you, whatever happened could be fixed. The man sounded like he was drowning with the fish. He loves you. And I mean in a love-love you way."

She smiled. It was true. Once she let go of the doubts, she believed he loved her, no matter who came into their lives.

"I changed my mind," she said. "I'm not calling him."

"What?" Angie said, moving closer. "I thought—"

"No, you thought right. I love him, and he loves me. But I'm not calling him." She punched in the number for her travel agent and held the phone to her ear. "I'm going through with our plans, and I'm flying to Washington. Can you all take me to the airport?"

All four of them smiled and nodded. She wrapped her arm around her stomach, holding in the excitement threatening to consume her. She still had to make things right with Bruce, but they'd be together. That's all that mattered.

Chapter Eighteen

A crowd of over two thousand spectators gathered three people deep along the western shores of Moses Lake. Bruce stood, ankle deep, in the water beside the sixteen-foot-trolling boat. The other competitors had left at the sound of the buzzer five minutes ago.

"What do you mean, Angie's on her way home? She and the other girls are supposed to be with Crista. I told Shauna to call me, and she hasn't. She knew I was busy, and I wanted someone to stay with Crista until I knew she was okay." Bruce switched hands and held the phone to his other ear to continue talking with Gary. "Call Juan or Grayson and have them find out what is going on."

"Grayson's having his own troubles. He's running a clinic for the junior league and Kate—Shauna's friend who usually watches Trevor when both of them are busy—is in bed with morning sickness. Grayson had to take the kid on the court with him. He doesn't have time to talk with anyone today," Gary said.

"What about Juan?" Bruce reached for the boat as it began to drift away. "Maybe he's heard from Dana."

"Tried, man. His calls are going to voicemail," Gary said. "Listen, you need to go do your thing. Let Crista do her thing. When you're finished, then you can worry about her. She's a big girl ... she doesn't need you holding her hand."

"This isn't any other girl. It's Crista," he muttered.

"I know, and she'd kick your ass if you threw a competition. Go win," Gary said. "I'll catch back up with you later and in the meantime, I'll see what I can do about finding out more."

"Yeah. Thanks." He disconnected the call and shoved the phone in his shorts pocket.

Ignoring all the curious gazes and the head shaking from the officials, he grabbed on to the side of the boat and hurled himself inside. He checked his watch. *Shit.*

He only had five minutes until the whistle blew to cut the motor and designate his spot on the lake. In quick concession, he drove the boat out to the southwest corner of the lake, hoping he hadn't already lost the number one spot he'd scouted last year during the fall. There was just enough debris in the water to create a hiding ground for wide mouth bass with enough shade to make the bass curious. He hoped to tempt the fish out into the sunshine with little effort.

The air horn from the judges' table on shore echoed over the surface of the water. He cut off the outboard motor and let the momentum of the boat push him toward the sheltered shoreline where a canopy of towering alder trees stood. While he grabbed his tackle box, he scanned the area around him. At least a dozen boats, scattered anywhere from twenty-five to one hundred feet from each other, were right in view of watching his every move. He'd have stiff competition this year because everyone wanted to take out the current champion.

He recognized Bill Kingston, fishing for Superior, Steven Longley representing Big Bear, and last year's second place winner, Greg Dermont. Adrenaline fueled him forward. He loved the challenge, the isolation, the need to be the best.

Using crank bait on his hook, he cast the line, leaving fifteen feet of release. He moved into motion with a pitching and flipping technique, hoping he'd guessed right and all he had to do was lure the motherfuckers out of hiding.

Lost in the moment, he appreciated the calm water, the light cool breeze in the ninety degree air, and forced himself to ease back on his worry over Crista. Gary was right. She was a grown woman, an independent person. How many times had she told him how much it meant to her to train and earn her own way without any sponsors, unlike in other sports? While most athletes sought backing, she bucked the system and achieved her goals all alone. He had a feeling most of that was because she'd learned at a young age if she wanted anything, she'd have to earn every penny. Her divorced parents, while a constant in her life, were not supportive of her. They believed she had lofty plans and would be better off getting married or working at the timber mill where they had spent most of their lives working for each paycheck, or having a couple of kids.

He flicked his wrist, brought tension to the line, and slowly reeled in the bait to try again. Water splashed along his shoulder from the pole, and he set the equipment against the seat of the boat and took off his T-shirt while he fished. Someday, he'd take Crista out on a lake like this and show her how to relax. She'd always enjoyed herself when he took her out fishing or at least was content to give him time to throw a few lines.

While she'd found it exciting in the ocean catching the halibut, it was salt water. His life was out here with fresh water, stocked lakes, and quiet.

He checked his watch. Twenty-four hours had passed since he last saw Crista, and it felt like a lifetime. He cast his pole. Giving Crista space when something was bothering her was not going to happen after today. Whether he won the tournament or lost, he had a private plane waiting to take him back to Cali to bring Crista home.

The hell with his schedule; he'd settle anything that troubled her. Then they'd join everyone else in Cottage Grove in a week and celebrate their togetherness before he was due to travel again. He blew out his breath and eased the tension in his shoulders. Gary was right. Shauna, Angie, Dana, and Diana would stay with Crista if she needed them. If Angie was on her way home that meant Crista was okay.

With the reassurance Crista would be okay, he sat straighter and whipped his line over the water. He missed her and couldn't wait to go get her. He'd overstepped a boundary he had no clue was there, and that tripped him up, but damned if he'd stand back and make her move all by herself. It was a man's job to provide for his woman. He wanted to take care of her for the rest of her life. She'd have to learn to let him.

The reel on his fishing pool spun. He put his finger along the line, pinching the slack, and the noticeable strong tug he needed came in rapid beats under his touch.

"That's it, you son-of-a-bitch," he muttered.

He waited, cooling his impatience, and when the line zipped through his fingers, he jerked the pole, setting the hook. "That's what I'm talking about."

More than the patience of waiting for a fish to take a bite, he played judge and jury by the fight of the bass at the end of his line. From experience, he knew it was worth taking his time, reeling it in, letting the fish wear itself out until it gave up. His fingers curled on the fishing pole, knowing his control allowed the fish to wage a fair fight.

At that exact moment, clarity came.

He knew exactly what he'd done to Crista.

He'd treated her like a big mouth bass.

Because she was his best friend and he'd skipped the flirting, the romance, the getting to know each other better in the natural progression of dating, he'd pushed his way into her life and forgot to take his time, reeling her in, letting her wear herself out until she came to him willingly.

How stupid could he be?

The line went slack. He changed hand positions and reeled the fish in before the hook could slip out. Working his way to the end of the boat, he leaned over the bow, keeping pressure on the line, and slipped his thumb through the fish's mouth.

Then he smiled. The tournament was over for him. He'd caught the motherfucker.

Even if someone outdid him, he'd take the hit because he had something more important to do than pick up a check and add another championship to his name.

He dumped the fish in the cooler of fresh water so as not to alter its size. Sweat beaded his forehead, and he shook his head. Time to go tell Crista he fucked up and start the rest of his life.

His cell phone vibrated. He reached in his pocket, noted the call came from Gary, swiped the keypad, and put the phone to his ear. "Hey, have you heard anything about Crista yet?"

"Yeah, man, and it isn't good," Gary said.

"What happened?" Bruce's balance wavered, and he stumbled back and plopped on the seat. "Is she okay?"

"I don't know. Angie isn't talking to me, and all the rest of the girls are home. I called Grayson, but he said Shauna picked up Trevor and left the club before he could speak with her," Gary said.

"That doesn't make sense," he muttered. "Let me talk to Angie."

"Uh, no, man. Can't do that. She'd kill me if she knew I was passing that much information over to you. You know how they can keep a secret and are always ragging on us for talking." Gary sighed. "But now I'm concerned, and before I wasn't."

He cupped his forehead. "For fuck's sake, tell me why."

"I heard—let's make this clear that I overheard because Angie didn't exactly tell me or know I was listening—her talking on the phone. Crista skipped town by herself and from the sound of it, she's hurting and Angie thinks leaving is the right thing to do. I'm sorry."

"She left Cali alone?" he muttered.

"Yeah, that's what I'm understanding," said Gary. "If I learn more, I'll call with an update."

Bruce lowered the phone and disconnected the call. Crista had left him.

She'd refused to talk and pushed him away, and now he had no way of knowing where the hell she'd go. He'd stripped her of everything she owned in his need to have her living with him, and all she had left was two weeks' worth of clothes. The whole situation was his fault.

How could she take care of herself when he had all her belongings sitting in the driveway of his house? She was away from everything and everyone she knew. Worst of all, she was hurting. How was he supposed to fix whatever bothered her and make her happy again?

The buzzer rent the air, signaling the end of the competition. He moved over to the outboard and started the motor. He ignored the other boats, the competitors, and the rules about passing on the right and made a straight shot to the shore. Time was running out on more things than winning. He had to find Crista before it was too late.

Chapter Nineteen

The loud buzzer signaled to the crowd that the event ended and to come to the judges' stands for the final inspection as the fishermen and fisherwomen came ashore. All the fans started talking at once, pulling out their binoculars, and trying to guess the outcome of the tournament by the expressions on the fishermen's faces. Crista raised her hand, shielding the glare coming off the water from the sun. She had no idea what boat Bruce was on or which direction he'd come from.

She dropped her arm, stepped back, and cupped her elbows, bouncing on her toes in her excitement at seeing him again. Last night, she'd arrived late to the motel and paid for her own room, knowing Bruce needed his sleep for today's tournament. What she planned to do to make up for being a demanding and—she swallowed hard—insecure woman would hopefully make up for her rash assumption that Bruce had thrown her to the curb for Janelle the first chance he had.

She was also nervous. What if she stepped over some boundary that Bruce had when he was in a relationship? She had no idea about his level of commitment or how he expected his girlfriend to act. She wanted more than their friendship, but she was clueless on all the little details.

"Here they come," said a man standing to her left.

Her stomach flip-flopped. Out of her element, she stepped back, letting the fans have their moment to witness the judging. Besides, she wanted Bruce's attention when they were alone and he deserved the spotlight today without being distracted.

"What the hell are you doing here?" said a man's voice behind Crista.

She glanced over her shoulder. At the sight of Bruce's manager, Dwayne, who she'd met a couple of times before, she pointed at her chest. "Are you talking to me?"

"Yes." He frowned. "Bruce almost missed the tournament because he was looking for you. He wasted fifteen minutes getting into place on the lake and wouldn't listen to me. For all I know, he threw the competition and it's your fault. Do you know what will happen if he begins to lose his ranking as the world-class bass fisherman? He'll sink. He can kiss his teaching seminars goodbye and every invite from other countries to fish their waters. He'll be miserable."

She shook her head and opened her mouth to explain, but Dwayne was right. She'd come between Bruce and his career, and that was unforgiveable. He loved competing even more than she loved doing the Ironman. It wasn't an individual goal for him the way it was with her. He fished because it relaxed him, it drove him to be better, and it brought him peace.

"I'm sorry," she whispered, turning away and walking back to her rental car.

"Make sure you stay away until he has private time to talk with you," Dwayne called after her.

There was a reason why she avoided relationships. Boyfriends interrupted her training. They also demanded more time than she was willing to give up to pursue a happily ever after. Why would she think it was any different for Bruce? He had more at stake and a career to lose.

Numb and confused, she cut through the crowd of vehicles in the parking lot. Just because she was willing to ease back and settle on training others after her last participation in the Ironman, giving her more time to concentrate on a relationship, didn't mean Bruce wanted to devote time to her. Maybe he believed they'd get together on the odd times they were both free.

"Shit," she muttered, rubbing her forehead. She knew better than to bring personal life to an event.

She dug her keys out of her pocket and opened the car. Her talk with Bruce could wait.

"Hey," Bruce yelled.

She whirled around and searched the crowd. Her heart raced, and her have-patience-and-wait lecture was a thing of the past.

A loud whistle drew her attention and she spotted Bruce standing half a body above the crowd, on top of something she couldn't see because of all the people crowding around him. She waved and pointed to her car. He'd know she was here and could find her at the motel.

He whistled again and the crowd grew silent. "Come here."

She shook her head, tapped her wrist, and pretended she wore a watch, hoping he knew she wanted him to meet her later.

"Damn it, get over here, sweetheart," he said, pointing to the ground at his hidden feet.

She covered her mouth and smiled stupidly. He was bossy and she loved him because he expected her to listen to him. She began walking, unable to turn down such a request.

The crowd parted at Bruce's demand, which made her laugh, and she dropped her hand from her mouth. She gazed at Bruce, feeling like she hadn't seen him in a year, instead of yesterday, and knowing she'd do anything in her power to make sure she never missed another day with him.

Bruce jumped down from the judge's table he was standing on, and hooked her neck with his hand, drawing her closer. He kissed her hot and heavy, and she lost her breath. Clutching his arms, she opened her mouth and received a small taste of him in return.

The fans surrounding them clapped. She pulled her lips away, and face planted in his chest, embarrassed she'd taken him away from his people. Yet, unashamed that right now, she couldn't muster up any guilt for taking his attention. Bruce's hand went down her arm, over her wrist, and he twined his fingers with hers. She followed along as he led her toward the water. When he stopped at the water's edge and picked her up, she threw her arms around his neck, unquestioningly. She'd go anywhere with him and trusted him completely.

"Coldwell," Dwayne said, running up to them. "Get back to the judges' table. They're going to announce the winner and dammit, you need to be there."

Bruce sat Crista in the boat, walked back the few feet to the shore, pulled back his fist, and punched his manager. Crista careened forward and caught herself on the bow of the boat. Shocked, she could only stare at Dwayne lying in the sand, holding his jaw.

"You're fired," Bruce said.

Dwayne shook his head and blinked. "What for?"

"What you said to Crista got back to me a split second after it happened. You ever blame Crista for interrupting my life again and you'll be doing more than picking yourself off the sand," Bruce said. "She comes first, always."

"Okay." Dwayne struggled to get his feet under him. "Fine. I'll remember that."

Bruce flexed his fingers on his right hand. "I'll have the final check for your services mailed to you tonight."

"Wait." Dwayne stumbled and righted himself. "I apologize. We can work this out."

Bruce shook his head. "If it was me you were dealing with, you'd get a second shot. But you're dealing with Crista, and I won't put up with you ever making her doubt her place in my life. We're finished."

Oh. My. God. Crista sat down on the bench in the boat. She was both appalled and screaming silently in joy. No one had ever defended her honor or punched someone out to protect her.

Bruce turned around and walked through the water to catch the boat that had slowly drifted away from shore. He gathered the loose rope and tossed it inside the bow and then jumped inside with her.

"Uh, Bruce … " She shifted closer to him, staying on the rocking seat. "Thank you, but you need to stay and finish the judging."

The corner of his mouth lifted. "Sweetheart, I don't have to do anything I don't want to do."

She sucked in her bottom lip and bit down. God, he was sexy.

The microphone squelched. She laid her hand on Bruce's leg, and he paused. She turned her gaze to the judges standing by the long line of bass strung up on the scales and marked with fluorescent marker tabs.

An older man tapped the mic. "We're proud to announce the champion for this year's Moses Lake Tournament, representing the entire Northwest Bass fisherman title is … reigning champion, Bruce Coldwell, with a thirty-one-and-a-half inch—"

"Are you ready now?" Bruce squeezed her hand. "Because I don't need all these people around when I want to kiss you … and I'm not talking about the way I kissed you back on shore in front of everyone."

She inhaled swiftly, pleasure swirling around in her stomach. She nodded, desperate for that kiss. "I'll go anywhere with you."

Bruce paused and studied her. Then he tilted back his head and laughed. The sound curled her toes and she held on for the ride out onto the lake. "Promise me one thing," she yelled over the roar of the motor.

"What?" he mouthed.

"Promise me we can talk first." She scrunched up her nose. "What I have to say is important, and if you touch me, I'll forget what I was going to say."

He winked and sped up the boat. She gazed out over the water and hoped that what she had to tell him would make sense. There was always the chance that he wouldn't understand. Or in his overconfident way, he'd see her insecurities as a weakness.

Chapter Twenty

The boat drifted in the middle of the lake after Bruce cut the engine. Crista swiped the stray hair off her cheek and gazed around the area. No one was out on the lake.

The other boats were still lined up along the shore, and the crowd remained behind to inspect the fish that were caught by the professionals, talk to the athletes, and get autographs from their favorite fisherman and fisherwoman. Crista finally had Bruce to herself.

Bruce sat across from her on the bench and leaned forward, bracing his elbows on his knees. She ogled his broad, bare chest, his long shorts clinging to his tanned legs, the tan she knew cut off low on his hips and began again above his knees. She'd teased him about his outdoorsman tan for years and the paleness of his thighs that never saw daylight. Not any longer because the absolute adorableness of a man who fished for a living was sexy, tan marks and all.

He was more sexy than she'd ever imagined, and whatever he did and the more she discovered the little intricacies about him—namely, the way he battled for her—endeared him to her even more.

"You wanted to talk … " He tilted his head, bringing her attention back to his face. "I'll admit that I don't feel like talking because it doesn't matter what went on in your head—you're here, with me, where you belong."

She melted. "It matters to me, though."

"Fair enough," he said, rubbing his hands along his thighs. "What's on your mind?"

"First off, you shouldn't have punched and fired your manager. Showing up here today and causing you trouble, not to mention my pushing you away from me in Cali, was my fault, and Dwayne had a right to be upset. Your career comes first, and I—I made a huge mistake and it could've cost you the tournament," she said.

He shook his head. "It's more than that, sweetheart. I won't allow anyone to upset you or put you second in my life. If that's an issue that's going to come between us, I'm afraid I won't budge."

"No, I like it, I think. I've never had someone who was willing to put me first before," she said. "I'm finding out a lot about myself, though, and not all of it's good. That's why I asked you to leave yesterday morning. I'm so sorry. I should've told you what was bothering me, but at the time, I was hurt. My whole world blew up over a stupid phone call, and all I can do to excuse what I did is tell you at that moment it was the most painful feeling I'd ever experienced."

He scooted forward and sprawled his hands on her bare thighs. "I'm not following you. What phone call?"

She thought about ending the conversation and retreating back to being the strong woman she portrayed to everyone who knew her, even Bruce. She even thought about omitting how Janelle made her feel because she detested how she lowered herself to worry about another woman. But the truth would get in the way of them moving forward, eventually. The threat could come as one of his fans, one of her friends, and Bruce had people in his life who loved him.

"I went out for a ride happy and feeling loved. You prepared ahead of time for me to have a phone on me, and even though I usually find your overbearing and protective tendencies a little irritating, I realized I quite liked how getting the phone made me feel." She waited to see if he'd say anything and when he remained quiet and listening, she continued. "I was almost at the end of my ride, and I got a flat tire. It happens all the time, but this time, I'd forgotten to pack the spare in my frame. For the first time, I learned the benefits of having a phone with me."

"That's what it was all about," Bruce said, thrumming his thumb along her skin. "I only want you to be safe."

She nodded. "I called you the morning I got the flat."

He frowned and the lines at the corner of his eyes intensified. She inhaled deeply. Her confession wasn't about making him feel bad. She had to come clean.

"I phoned my apartment because I knew you'd be there, and Janelle answered the phone." She moistened her lips. "I found out that you'd asked her over and that you were too busy to come to the phone ... at least that's what Janelle told me. My mixed thoughts collided together over hearing her voice, and yours in the background, and I knew that you'd picked Janelle over me the first chance you got."

"I didn't—"

"I know." She hurried and said, "After I asked you to leave, and after the girls came to talk me down from killing Janelle, I realized the truth when I went over and bitched out Janelle and warned her away from you. I was jealous. I'm insecure around other women who are feminine and beautiful. They know how to handle men and relationships. All I know how to do is breathe through the adrenaline stage and to push myself into a zone to perform the best endurance possible, so I can prove I'm as good or better than everyone else."

"Okay, you're done talking." He pulled her over onto his lap and wrapped his arms around her. "You're better than all the other women, and I'll prove it to you every day. I get what you're saying, and I understand why you felt you needed to warn me about your jealous streak, but sweetheart, I love you for who you are."

"Even now?" she asked, feeling the warmth from both the sun and his words.

He chuckled, sinking his face into her hair and breathing deeply. "Even more now. You're beautiful, sexy, and everything I've ever wanted. I don't want other women. I want you."

Her whole body tingled and she slipped her arm around his back and held on to him. The feelings circling her body were not the friend status ones, but the all-consuming, she'd never leave him ones, even if he tried to push her away kind.

"Just to warn you, I probably won't like any of your female friends," she mumbled against his neck. "Or any woman that looks at you."

"Okay." His chest rumbled in amusement. "I can deal with that."

"Also, you might want to continue being the badass boyfriend who punches other men in the face for hurting my feelings." She lifted her chin and put her lips on his ear. "That's really hot."

"I'll remember that," he whispered, caressing the curve of her hip. "Do you have anything against having sex with me on the boat, out in the middle of the lake?"

She shook her head. "Can anyone see us out here?"

"We'll keep our asses below the side of the boat," he said, hooking his thumb in the waistband of her shorts. "They won't see a thing."

He rose from the seat and lowered her to the floor , pushing tackle bags and fishing poles out of the way. She squealed as a pool of cold water hit her lower back. Then she laughed as Bruce pulled off his shorts and she found him naked underneath. Her man went commando, and she loved it.

She rolled to the side, letting him soak up the water with the clothes he'd removed and then grabbed the shorts off the seat to cushion her head from the hardness of the aluminum.

"Your fans probably have their binoculars and big ass zoom lenses on their cameras trained right on your white butt," she said, smiling at him.

He straightened his shoulders, posing in all his glory, and she laughed softly in amusement. Cocky, pure cocky, and she loved that about him. He had enough security for the both of them.

She lifted her hips and peeled her shorts and panties down her legs. Peeking over the side of the boat, she hurried and stripped off her tank and bra. Used to the coolness of the boat and heated from the inside because of Bruce loving her, she lay down and held out her hand. The thrill of outdoor sex for the first time and sharing the moment with Bruce excited her.

He lowered himself down beside her. His warm flesh had her rolling to her side to share his heat. His palm moved from the swell of her hip to the hollow of her waist then grazed her ass. She ran her hand over his shoulder, never wanting him to stop. Her nipples constricted and she ended up rolling onto her back to let him touch more of her. She needed him to consume every spot on her body.

He bent his free arm and supported his head on his hand, while he took his sweet time with his other hand, exploring her body, leaving no part of her out. She quivered as he trailed his hand up her thigh and around to the flat of her stomach and between her breasts, lingering at the plumpness on the outer edges.

His gaze followed his movements, and she enjoyed watching the fascination, the lust, the heat filling his eyes. Finally, he moved his hand downward, skimming her pubic bone, her inner thighs. She spread her legs, greedy for his touch and hungry to have him deep inside of her. But he continued his slow exploration as if memorizing every curve, every valley, on her.

"You are the most beautiful woman in my world, sweetheart." His voice was deeper, more sincere than she'd ever heard, and she believed him.

She leaned up and kissed him, a slow mesh of lips, graduating to tasting each other. Her pussy dampened with the erotic caress of his tongue. She threw her leg over his thigh and pressed her breasts, aching and tender, into his chest. His hardness pressed against her lower stomach and the gentle throbbing grew harder.

Her pelvis arched in lazy dips and rises against him, trying to ease the pressure building inside of her.

In a heartbeat, Bruce was above her, kneeling in the boat between her thighs, his hands on each side of her, and his gaze locked on hers. "Condom in my shorts."

She raised her brows. "Mr. Convenient, huh?"

"When I'm with you, damn straight." He sucked in a breath as she put the condom on him.

He entered her with a patient slowness as if they had all the time in the world. She loved his ability to slow her down to savor the experience when all she wanted to do was go wild because she knew how good it was with him.

He lowered his head and kissed her again. She lifted her arms and circled his neck, holding him in place, afraid he'd stop and delighted when he thrust all the way inside of her, stealing her breath. Because this was Bruce, he took control and she happily let him.

His movements grew faster, and she moaned into his mouth. She needed to move, to feel more of him, to plunge herself against him. Her near climax spiraled low and deep between her legs, and he slowed, dragging the delicious torture out, not letting her go over the edge, but building her higher.

He cupped the back of her head with his hand and brought his thrusts to the surface, barely touching her, dipping his cock and quickly pulling away. She squirmed under him, trying to take more of his length.

"So beautiful, sweetheart," he mumbled, kissing her again.

He plunged deep once more, drawing a louder moan from her. She reached for the next stroke, and it never came. He went back to teasing her, touching her, denying her, making her crazy with need. His tongue fluttered against her lips, and she nipped him.

He growled and sank his cock into her sex, burying himself to his balls. Again and again, deeper and faster. *Oh, God.*

He set a rhythm that had her pussy spasming, her legs stiffening, and her core dancing. Only the sound of her breathing and an occasional bird whistling as it flew overhead invaded their moment. Bruce took her to the most beautiful place where sunlight shined upon her soul, and her world rocked in sensual pleasure.

Tireless and determined, Bruce continued his exquisite torture. Her climax came and flooded her with the most marvelous intensity. She wrapped herself around him, pulsing with each contraction of pleasure.

"Yes, yes … " She clung to him as his body shuddered its own release.

Several minutes passed, and then Bruce rolled off her to the side, pillowing her head on his chest, his arm around her, and blew out his breath. She smiled against his skin.

"I love you," she whispered.

"Love-love?" His arms tightened.

She nodded. "Yeah, I love-love you."

"Love-love you more," he whispered back.

She closed her eyes, sure that anything he was feeling, she felt ten times more. She had everything she'd ever wanted—her best friend and the man she'd love forever.

"We've got six days before we're due in Cottage Grove," he said.

She sighed, not ready to share him with others quite yet. "I know."

"But before we go there, I want to take you somewhere else." He pulled her into a sitting position. "Crista?"

She moistened her lips. "Yeah?"

"We're getting married." He heaved himself off the bottom of the boat and stood, naked and unconcerned that his fans on shore could see him. "It'll be a rush job. We'll fly to Vegas. I'll buy you a ring, and then I'll buy you a ring every year on our anniversary to make up for every gag gift I've ever bought you in the past."

He tossed her the clothes she'd had on before they had sex. She thrust her arms into her shirt and leaned back to shove her legs in her shorts. When she had them over her hips she stood and zipped them up. "Are you kidding me?"

"Serious, sweetheart. I'm not wasting any more time." He looked at her. "You have a problem with that?"

Drunk with happiness, she smiled. "Nope. I'm good with getting married."

"Great." He leaned over and kissed her. "We're going to have a great life together."

"Yeah," she said, bursting with love for the only man who could sweep her off her feet and make damn sure she was along for the ride.

Bruce started the boat motor and the movement took her back down. She caught herself on the seat and watched Bruce guide the boat, going faster than she knew was legal on the lake, and smiled. She was getting married, and she couldn't be happier.

Chapter Twenty-One

The makeshift chapel in the House of Elvis played "Blue Suede Shoes" on a CD that sounded worse than the three guys singing in harmony on the Vegas sidewalk when they'd arrived an hour ago. Crista grinned at Bruce, not caring that none of their friends were here to witness their marriage. The only thing she needed was him, the marriage certificate—which she held in her hand—land the two hundred dollar ring they'd bought in the gift shop, along with an "I Had Sex in Vegas" T-shirt she'd pulled over her tank to wear on her wedding day.

Bruce's mouth softened. "Looking pretty hot, Mrs. Coldwell."

"So are you, Mr. Coldwell," she said.

He was in sneakers, surfer shorts, and a plain white T-shirt with a small logo of a mysterious fishing company over the left part of his chest. They'd both agreed that they weren't the type of people to dress up for twenty minutes when they both had plans to run back to their room and get naked.

"You know, they have a room we can rent behind the stage by the hour." He winked.

She nudged him with her arm. "Not on your life. I'm not having sex for the first time after tying the knot in a place where Elvis is probably videotaping the sacred union for an extra thirty-five dollars."

Bruce pulled her into his side. "Then let's go, sweetheart. We've got a honeymoon to start and we've got four days to wear ourselves out."

They walked the block back to the hotel, Crista holding his hand and practically floating in her sneakers. At the electronic doors, Bruce swept her up into his arms. She squealed. "What are you doing?"

"Carrying you over the threshold," he said, stepping into the building.

She wrapped her arms around his neck and kicked her feet in amusement. "I think you could've waited until we got up to the fifth floor."

"Nope. If I'm going to play, I'm playing big." He marched through the lobby to the catcalls of the other guests. "This will be a day we'll remember for the rest of our lives."

He was creating memories. Crazy, unforgettable memories and letting her experience a side of life she'd never had time to explore. Her life since falling in love-love with Bruce consisted of chaos and surprises. She had no idea what tomorrow would bring, but none of that mattered because she was exactly where she wanted to be.

A gentleman from the hotel held the elevator door open for them. She smiled her thanks from her perch in Bruce's arms. The ride upstairs took no time, and then the next thing she knew, she was flat on her back on the bed and Bruce was stripping off his clothes. Not to be outdone, she took off her new shirt, her bra, her shorts, and panties, and was retrieving a condom out of the bedside drawer when the mattress dipped from Bruce's weight when he joined her on the bed.

He had her underneath him as soon as she'd ripped open the package. She palmed him, finding him hard and wanting. With a practiced hand, she put the protection on his erection in record time. He fisted her hair and positioned her head. The forbidden pain on her scalp delighted her. She loved sex rough and hard as much as she liked to make love slow and gentle. With Bruce, he gave her everything to meet her needs.

His mouth came down on hers. She was right where she wanted to be. There was no thought to protest or to change positions because she wanted him there, pressing down on her, his hand holding her, and his mouth on her lips.

She opened her mouth and his tongue slipped inside. Her body melted as he stroked her. She curved her hand around his neck, holding him there, kissing him back, giving and taking. She no longer thought about what they were doing and who she was with. Everything was perfect.

She kissed him greedily. Without delay, he leaned against her. Her breath came fast, already turned on. The moment he'd said *I do*, she wanted him again. She scratched at his shoulders and arched her hips off the bed, eliciting a growl from Bruce. A tremor went through her sex, spiraling in her lower belly. God, he was sexy.

Half wild, half tamed, and fully skilled in bed, he knew exactly what made her wet for him.

He moved to the left, putting his hand over her breast. She pressed into his hold, loving the way her body tingled for him. His fingers pinched, twisted. It was rough, but dazzling. She was not a weak woman. She trained hard and she was strong, but Bruce made her feel feminine and loved with his demands. Her hips rose in an impulsive demand.

"Honey," she whispered, needing him inside of her. She moved her hand from his hair to his shoulder and down his arm, searching for his hand. "Please."

He entwined their fingers, pressing her into the mattress. His mouth found her lips again. She moaned against his tongue, bucking her hips.

He didn't hesitate. His cock pressed against her sex. The ache deep inside of her grew, and she wanted every inch of him, body and soul.

"Beautiful." He groaned debd drove in deep.

She gasped and held her breath until she grew lightheaded from the power of their bodies joined together. When she exhaled, he moved, filling her again and again, rough, hard, almost impatient. She panted. Her body was spiraling, tightening, reaching.

Her hand squeezed his fingers and she wrapped her legs around his hips, digging her heels into his ass to leverage her hips. "Yes."

Pleasure built fast, and she could feel her orgasm coming. She was burning up and yet chills rolled over the surface of her skin. He touched a part of her that she'd never known existed until him. A primal need to be loved that only he could validate, and make her believe he worshiped her.

He kissed her again. Her body clenched, and she tore her mouth from his, arched her neck, her back, and let out a hoarse, breathy moan. "Bruce."

Bruce's hips sped up. In. Out. In. Out.

That's when pleasure hit her. The intensity of the first spasm shook her body and she tightened her limbs around him, pulling him closer.

He thrust while she came in the most powerful and unequivocal shower of awesomeness. As she came down from her high, his thrusts became even stronger. He once again sank his hand into her hair and captured her mouth. She tightened her legs and he groaned, his hips drove into her once, twice, and then he planted himself all the way inside her and stopped.

His mouth slid from hers, down her chin, and to her neck, where he buried his face against her skin and shuddered his release. She lay underneath him, taking his weight, and holding him.

He rolled off her, taking her with him. She trailed her fingers over his damp shoulder before wrapping her arms around him and felt her love for him grow. She had a feeling they were just at the tip of discovering each other, even though they'd been best friends for so many years.

"I love-love you, sweetheart," he said.

She smiled at him, wanting to tell him how much he meant to her, but he already knew. So, she said simply, "I love-love you, too, honey."

Chapter Twenty-Two

Four days later in Cottage Grove, California.

In Grayson and Shauna's living room, Crista reached out and snagged Bruce's hand. She held on to him as her friends gave her the evil eye. No matter how many times they yelled at her for leaving them out of their plans and not inviting them all to the wedding, she wouldn't change one thing about her and Bruce's impulsive trip to Las Vegas prior to coming to Cottage Grove.

"Because you ripped us off on celebrating your wedding, I'm going to have to throw you a huge party." Shauna pulled out her phone and tapped the screen. "How about the last day of the month? It's a Saturday. Everyone can stay here at the house, and whoever doesn't fit can room over at Diana's bed and breakfast."

Crista squeezed Bruce's hand and shook her head. "That won't work. We're heading home to Bruce's house in Oregon—"

"Yes. I get them." Dana clapped.

Bruce's house was nowhere near Dana and Juan's chalet by Mt. Hood, but the two-hour trip was short enough from the coast; they were practically neighbors in the same state. Crista smiled at her friend. She'd find some excuse to stay in contact now that she was married.

"We don't want to push it into November because Dominic won't be able to get away. That also means Diana will be with Dominic, and … " Shauna scrolled through her calendar. "We'll do October."

"Actually, we can't do it then, either." Crista inhaled and straightened her shoulders. "I've got the Ironman. It'll be my last one, and I'll be announcing my retirement after I cross the finish line."

Everyone at the Schyler house quieted. Bruce dropped her hand and put his arm around her. She leaned against him. The news shocked everyone, but she wanted her friends to hear first.

"I've been planning this decision for a long time. Quitting this year has nothing to do with Bruce and me falling in love and marrying," she said. "Thanks to Juan—" she smiled around Bruce at Juan "—and his connections, I've been hired on to train the triathlons on the U.S. Olympic team."

Cheers of congratulations deafened her and she accepted hugs from Dana, Shauna, Diana, Angie, and a very pregnant Kate who'd brought her husband, Jackson, to the get together. Gary was the first of the guys to approach her.

Crista held out her arms, needing one thing from Gary to know he understood. "If you don't do it, I'll know you disapprove of my decision."

Gary stepped toward her, wrapped his arms around her, and lifted her high in the air in one of his famous bear hugs. She squeaked, gasping for breath, but her hands pressed in on his back, returning the hug. These were her friends, and she was glad that they'd continue being in her and Bruce's life.

After Gary set her on her feet, Grayson kissed her cheek and mumbled congratulations. Juan shook her hand, pulling her in for a one arm hug that had her swaying to keep her balance. Finally, Dominic clapped his broad hands on her shoulders and peered down at her.

"Proud of you," he said, in a Russian accent so thick with emotion, she swallowed hard.

"Thanks, Dom," she said, reaching up on her tiptoes to kiss his cheek. "I'm proud of you, too."

He nodded without a flicker of a smile and said, "Of course you are."

She slugged his arm and laughed. His ego, bigger than anything his broad shoulders could carry, was a welcome reminder of her life. She was still one of them, the group of misfit athletes … but different, maybe better because now she love-loved one of the men in the group.

"Okay, that's it. Scratch the marriage celebration; we'll have a party whenever we can all get together again and call it good." Shauna lunged and scooped up a running Trevor. "What have you been in?"

Trevor's toothy grin showed through a face covered in chocolate. Crista bit her lip to keep from laughing because Grayson's eyes darted to Gary who looked away and rubbed the back of his neck. Earlier, she'd seen Gary set a bag of Dove's chocolate on the table and she suspected little Trevor had found the mother lode of candy.

Grayson walked over to his family. "I'll take him upstairs and clean him up."

"That's okay, I'll take him, and you can visit with your friends," Shauna said.

"Yeah, well, my friends are all big boys, and they'd understand that I want you upstairs, alone." Grayson turned Shauna around and guided her up the stairs with his hands on her hips amid a chorus of catcalls.

Crista's chest warmed. If Grayson and Shauna weren't fighting, they were having sex. She laid her head on Bruce's chest. Now that she thought of it, she hadn't seen them fight since six months ago when Shauna decided to dance on the table at Girl's Night Out. Not that it was strictly the girls anymore. Every one of the men came, too.

"So training, huh?" Juan leaned against the end of the couch, pulled Dana back into the V of his legs, and wrapped his arms around her stomach. "Won't you miss winning?"

"Honestly, I don't think so." She glanced up at Bruce. "At the last two Ironman events, the high never came the way it did at the beginning. Once I was done, it was more about what I could do to improve my technique and how to condition better. I've found that I get more enjoyment from the training aspect of it all and teaching others so they can reach their goals. I'm also getting old, and training hours each day is pushing me too hard."

Dominic coughed. "Twenty-six years old. Ancient."

"Twenty-seven." She looked at the other women in the room. "I'm the oldest female here, and look what each of them has done with her life. They're all married, business owners, event planners, a mother. I've only trained. It's—"

"It's Crista's time to enjoy life, have a family, and maybe if we're lucky, we can add another rug rat to the group to keep Trevor from being too spoiled." Bruce grinned and Crista swore his chest grew broader.

"I would like a family," she said softly.

Gary nodded. "What did your parents think of you getting hitched in Vegas?"

"Oh, you know, they were happy for me." Crista shrugged. "They told us to stop by sometime when we're in Idaho."

Gary's gaze softened and he nodded. He understood how she had to let the disappointment over her parents' lack of involvement go.

One drunk night, a few years ago, after she'd gone out with all the boys, Gary had been the ear to her troubles with her parents. She had known a little about his background being raised in foster care, and though he never shared any information with her, he'd let her talk until she'd fallen asleep. He knew how much her lack of parental pride bothered her.

"We've got news." Diana plopped down on Dominic's lap and wrapped her arms around his neck. "Does anyone want to take a guess?"

"You're pregnant?" Kate said, rubbing the roundness of her stomach where her own child grew.

"No. Not yet." Diana grinned. "During the month of August next year, we're shutting down the B&B and hosting the twelve kids that go to Grayson's tennis camp. We signed a contract last week. Schyler's Tennis Center has already outgrown the dorm building Grayson had constructed in the back of his property, so Grayson's going to let the kids he sponsors live it up at our place. I can't wait. We'll have a house full of kids to motivate and help further their dreams."

"That's awesome," Crista said.

If anyone could inspire kids, it was Dominic. He'd fought his way to the top of the hockey circuit from his beginnings as a poor, but much loved, kid from Russia. His quiet acceptance and positive speeches enthralled many children not to give up on their dreams.

"Well, we've got news too. We're pregnant," Juan blurted. "I mean Dana is."

Before they could react, Shauna jogged down the stairs and hugged Juan and Dana together. Crista waited her turn, and after all hugs and kisses were once again shared, she pulled Bruce to the side of the room.

"I need to catch my breath. Can we go outside for a few minutes?" she asked.

"Yeah, sweetheart." He led her by the hand out the front door.

Outside, she inhaled deeply, enjoying the fresh air. The last week had been a whirlwind of running here and there, getting married, setting up meetings, getting familiar with her new position, and most of all, getting used to being with Bruce every step of the way. She slipped her hand from his, and tucked her fingers in his back pocket.

"Everything okay?" he asked.

She smiled up at him. "Perfect. I just miss being with my husband."

"We could go back to the hotel in town and call it a night." He wiggled his brows. "Maybe skip out later for a dip in the pool."

"Hm. You did keep me from swimming my laps last night." She curled into him, until they were breasts to stomach. "Do you ever stop and notice that we've had a thing for water since the day where we scandalized all of Moses Lake?"

"My girl, water and a fishing pole, that's all I need." He kissed her lips lightly and mumbled, "And fish."

"Speaking of fish, I've been meaning to ask you what you did with that freezer full of halibut at my old apartment?" she asked.

"Nothing, why?" He brushed her hair off her shoulders.

She stiffened. "You didn't give it to the Fredricksons?"

"No," he said.

"Oh my God." She stepped back. "I unplugged the fridge and freezer when I left for the airport to meet you."

She covered her mouth and laughed. The more she tried to stop, the louder she became, until she was holding on to Bruce, wiping her cheeks dry on his T-shirt. Karma really was a bitch.

"Do you want to let me in on why a smelly freezer of fish is funny?" Bruce held her shoulders.

"I ... " She barked with laughter. "I called the manager at the apartment complex yesterday to give them my forwarding address to send me the tax papers I need to write off my classes I taught while I was living there ... "

"And?" he asked.

"Terry—that's the manager's name—informed me that Janelle had requested a move into my old apartment because she stated the air coming off the ocean was good for her complexion. He hates dealing with her, so he told her he'd wave the deposit if she cleaned my old apartment out herself." She pressed her hand on her chest. "She's going to get quite the surprise when she opens up the freezer and finds all the packages of thawed and rotted halibut."

Bruce stalked forward and pinned Crista between his body and the side of the porch. He kissed her thoroughly, paying attention to her lips, her tongue, her senses. The humor settled in her lower stomach and warmed. She tried to summon a little bit of guilt over Janelle's unfortunate mishap, but Bruce's attention made that impossible.

"You're an evil woman, sweetheart." He grinned.

"She deserves it," she said.

He pulled back. "Let's say goodnight to the others, and go back to the hotel."

"Yeah, I'm ready." She wiped the lipstick she'd put on for the occasion off the corner of his mouth. "I'm going to wear you down and win this time."

He threw back his head and laughed. "Only you would turn sex into a competition."

"You like what I do, honey." She smiled up at him as they walked to the front door. "I have to feed my competitive side somewhere now that I'm settling down."

He stopped before she could walk inside. "Anytime, anywhere, sweetheart."

She followed him into the house, sure that everyone knew why she was smiling, and not caring if they did. She had everything she'd ever wanted, including her best friend.

More from This Author
(From *Secretly* by Debra Kayn)

The gravel road crunched under the soles of Angie Swanson's Nike runners. The fierce wind blew off the mountain range and swept her honey-brown hair behind her shoulders. She stopped in the middle of Main Street and squinted into the setting sun, gazing down a barren, straight road.

Of all the places she never imagined herself ending up, it was Deadhorse, Oregon. Worse yet, she always dreamed she'd be working at a major spa, specializing in Swedish massage. Instead, she was the super pumper at her older brother Drew's gas station.

It was, in fact, The Gas Station. Drew couldn't even come up with a better name on the sign, despite her suggestions to glam it up into something more. Angie's Pumps, Octane in Lavender, or even leaning in the direction of hilarity with *Let us pump you up* would've been better than The Gas Station. Drew had rejected all of them for the nondescript, boring name; but that wasn't surprising. He lived in Deadhorse.

Dead. Horse.

She didn't belong here. The slow pace where people only talked about the weather and June Murphy's prized rose bushes outside the post office bored her to tears. To her, they were flowers. Red ones, that looked like any other rose bush in a million other front yards.

She had been born to do something big. Bigger than pumping gas in a deceased animal town where only the wind kept her company.

After spending four years at Washington State University, majoring in Journalism, she'd quickly learned after taking a community class on therapeutic massages that she wanted to change professions. So, she'd left her gopher position at the *Seattle Times*, and succeeded in landing a posh job at Le Massage. Then, three months ago, after working there almost two years, the spa closed. Unable to afford to keep renting the apartment she shared with her best friend, Jules, she'd taken up Drew's offer to work for him.

Temporarily, of course.

Every day, each longer and more depressing than the last, passed in a blur of mundane information overload, high-strung emotions, and the foolish realization that she should have bought stock in Doritos—for how much they were the main staple of her diet lately. Not to mention last week her father had dropped off her four-year-old half-sister and five-year-old half-brother for two days of fun with big sis while he vacationed with her stepmom. The past three months had been a painful lesson about living in Loserville.

She had to find a job before she lost the rest of her sanity. She glanced down at her sneakers and groaned. Seriously, what kind of place had cow shit in the middle of the road? Obviously there were some animals alive and kicking still around.

She dragged her foot behind her for ten paces, rechecked her sole, and declared it as clean as it'd get. Not that anyone would notice. The smell of gasoline on her clothes overrode *eau de toilette* poo.

Angie would give anything to escape and go back to Seattle. She sighed, gazing up into the sky. Whether it was because she'd hit rock bottom or simply because she wanted something better in her life than living her brother's dream, she'd started scouring the internet and applying for any job she qualified for. And still nobody hired her.

Something had to change soon. She sniffed, and raised her chin. The desire to ride the monorail and go shopping downtown at Nordstrom tempted her each day. But Seattle was twelve hours away. The price of gas alone was too much for her to rent a car to return to the Rose City to visit.

But until circumstances changed, she'd spend her free time pumping gas, washing windshields, and checking tire pressure. She hooked her thumbs in the front pockets of her shorts and walked back toward the gas station, which she'd closed an hour ago. With her brother gone to pick up another project car, she had to work alone. At least he was due back tomorrow, and she'd have someone to talk with during the day.

Distracted by the many things on her wish list, she gave the man leaning against the gas pump a cursory glance and opened her mouth to tell him the gas station was closed when recognition dawned on her. She gasped and covered her mouth.

Tall with huge shoulders, Gary Satchel, the Seattle Seahawks' wide receiver, hijacked her attention. She stood without saying a word, not believing he was here. But it was him. Not just anybody could pull off his size.

His well-worn Levi's, blue and silver Seattle Seahawks football jersey, six foot four inches tall with dark stormy eyes, the two inch scar running the length of his left cheekbone on his handsome face told her everything she needed to know. She raised her gaze and shouted in joy. Her brother's best friend had come to save her.

"Gary," she said on an exhale, launching herself into his arms.

He remained silent, as he was known to do. She closed her eyes, squeezing back the tears of relief at having his famous bear hug wrapping her tightly in his embrace. If there was one person she trusted, besides her brother, it was Gary.

He'd been the solid body she'd clung to during her teenage years when life seemed too cruel to handle alone. Later, he'd become her protector when drunk guys hit on her at the clubs. He always lent her an ear when she needed to talk, and he listened without judgment.

"Sorry to hear about the job, Ang." He inhaled deeply, expanding his chest; she could barely get her arms around him.

She leaned back so she could gaze up at his face. "They picked that asshole Rodden over me to go to Germany to open the new shop. Can you believe that? The guy's rough with his hands and has the bedside manners of a stuck-up prick. The least they could've done is keep the spa open here in Seattle, instead of closing. My clientele alone would've been enough to make it profitable."

He chuckled. "Asshole? Prick?"

"Drew's rubbing off on me. Shop talk—go figure." She shuddered. "What are you doing here?"

She reluctantly stepped away from him and forced her shoulders back. Glad to have someone she knew to talk with, she wasn't going to scare him off by bitching. He gave her hand one more squeeze before letting go.

"I thought I'd stay a couple days, see your brother, and pester you." He motioned for her to walk with him.

"I'm not even going to rise to the bait. I'm seriously lacking in any intelligent conversations. The only things people here talk about are hay prices and how many days until winter." She leaned closer and touched him again to make sure she wasn't hallucinating. "Besides, I get you all to myself. Drew's out on business and won't be home until tomorrow."

"Damn. I'd hoped he'd be around." He pointed to the restored Camaro in the driveway of Drew's house behind the garage. "I wanted to see if he could check the muffler. It's riding rough, and sounds like it's made for the racetrack."

"Ugh. Don't talk cars. That's all I hear about twenty-four/seven. Between the gas station and Drew, I've heard enough to last a lifetime." She walked up the driveway, and noticed his bags lying by the front door. "I am so glad you're here."

"Maybe I should hit the motel." He stopped and put his hand on his car. "I'll come by tomorrow and spend some time with you both."

"Are you crazy?" She grabbed his hand. "I just said this place is boring me to tears. Stay at the house and fill me in on what's happening in the Emerald City. Then I want to pick your brain about places I can send my résumé and—" she swallowed "—afterward, I want to hear what is going on with you."

"Same old thing. Training, meetings, and football." He winked. "What you should do is stay with your friend Jules while you search for a job, so you're in the city and closer to a bigger job market. Nowadays, you almost have to be the first one to apply to get the job and that requires being on location."

"I can't. I already asked her last month if she could do me a favor and let me mooch off her until I find employment. She can't do it. She needs a paying roommate in order to afford the rent." She pouted. "Besides, she's already found a roommate since I left…one with a job."

"Too bad."

She leaned into his arm. "I'm stuck here, unless you're looking to help a family friend out and don't mind having a roommate who can't afford to pay you for a few weeks."

"Absolutely not."

"But, Gary…" She gazed up at him and gave him the saddest, most pathetic look she could muster. "You wouldn't even see or hear me. I'll pay you the back rent once I land a job."

"No."

"I'll clean your house."

"Unlike you, I'm not messy." He laughed. "I don't need a maid."

She glared. "Come on, please?"

"No way." He shook his head. "I've got enough going on with my life. Pre-season practice starts in two weeks."

"Some friend you are. I'd let you stay here if you wanted." She snorted. "What a joke. This place would drive you insane in a week's time."

"Women. Never satisfied." He grunted and thumped the roof of the car as they walked by. "Let's go in the house. I'm beat, and the trip was killer."

Tears came to her eyes. This time she didn't have to fake them. Frustration boiled inside her. She was getting desperate enough to hide in his trunk on the way back to Seattle. Once they arrived, he'd have no choice but to let her stay in his mansion of a condominium.

"Give it up, Ang. The answer's no."

She followed him toward the house. "You don't know what I'm thinking."

"I do." He tugged a strand of her hair and looped it behind her ear. "I've known you too long."

"Whatever." She squeezed past him into the room.

Inside the one-story rambling ranch house, the living room sat in disarray. She'd littered the area with all her belongings, and hadn't found the energy to clean since Drew left a week ago.

There was a pillow and blanket thrown haphazardly on the couch, where she'd curled up to watch a movie in the middle of the night when she couldn't sleep. She hurried over and grabbed her things. Then she threw the contents on a pile of boxes near the fireplace.

"Sorry for the disaster zone." She kept her back turned to Gary, and pushed the box of books out of the middle of the living room. "I'll just move—" she grunted "—everything out to the garage."

"Leave it. I'll help you move everything later. Although, it seems messed up that Drew didn't at least get you situated in a bedroom. Are you sure you haven't killed him, or run him off his own property?" He gripped her shoulders, turned her around, and stared into her eyes. "Tell me you didn't drive him over the edge in three months?"

"No, but I'm taking that as a challenge." She grinned wickedly. "I bet that I can crack you in twelve hours."

"You're probably right." His smile disappeared, and he ran his hand over the top of a box. "So, why is all your stuff in the living room?"

"We moved everything out here when Dad dropped Willie and Desiree off here last week for a couple of days, and they took over my bedroom," she said. "I think my lil bro and sis brought every toy they owned with them."

"You love the chaos." He pointed to the couch. "Sit. Relax."

She plopped down on the couch. "I need excitement in my life that comes from people over the age of twenty-one."

"Well, don't wish too hard. A busy life gets old too." He scratched his chest. "Is there beer in the fridge?"

She shrugged. "I don't know. I haven't looked."

"When did you say Drew left?" He walked across the great room, opened the fridge, and pulled out two bottles of beer.

"Uh, five…six days ago." She rubbed her forehead. "Each miserable day is the same. I might've lost track."

"And you don't know what's in the fridge? What have you been eating?" He twisted the cap off both drinks and passed her one. "Here."

"Thanks." She held the drink in her lap, not lifting it to her mouth. "I eat…stuff."

"Dammit." He stalked back into the kitchen. "Get in here and sit your butt down at the counter."

She stood, walked over to the bar stool, and sat. "Why are you mad?"

"You need to eat wholesome food." He searched the cabinets, and took out a half loaf of bread and a jar of peanut butter. "You had no business jogging if you're not taking care of yourself. You'll make yourself sick—or pass out.

"I've eaten," she mumbled, raising the beer to her mouth.

"What?" He stared at her an extra beat. "Your usual junk?"

"If you have to know, I've eaten two bags of Doritos. Family size." She pointed to the empty bags on the counter. "Nacho flavored, which means there's cheese in it, so I'm getting my calcium."

"That's it?" He shook his head as he plunged a knife into the peanut butter.

"No. I also ate a few of those Little Debbie cupcakes, and the vending machines at The Gas Station have already-made sandwiches. The ham and cheese ones are pretty good." She lifted her chin. "You didn't come back here to complain about my diet, have you?"

"Eat this." He put the sandwich in front of her.

She wrinkled her nose. "I'm not hungry."

"Tough. You need some protein to restore your energy. You're practically dragging your feet." He opened the freezer and dropped a package of frozen meat on the counter. "When you're done with that you'll have a proper dinner."

Gary peeled the butcher paper away, and put a solid chunk of steaks on a plate in the microwave. Angie blinked. "I can't eat all that."

"Honey, only one of those is yours." He turned back around and winked. "It was a long trip, and I'm starving."

She smiled and a short laugh escaped. It was the first real happy sound that had come from her in over a week and surprisingly, it felt good; comforting.

"It's so nice to have you here." She leaned her elbows on the counter. "How long can you stay?"

"Well, here's the thing." He pulled a sack of potatoes out from under the sink. "I've got two days until I'm due for a press conference, so I'm spending the time here. I wish I would've called first, because I was really hoping to catch up with Drew. Between his work and my football, we struggle to get together on a regular basis."

She chewed the last bite of her sandwich, swallowed, and brushed the crumbs from her lips. "At least you'd get to see me almost weekly at the clubs…you know, if I was in Seattle."

"Stop trying to talk me into letting you stay with me." He looked away from her. "It wouldn't be a good idea."

He was hiding something from her. She knew him too well, and he'd been off his game since he'd arrived. More mellow and quiet. His usual easygoing attitude and teasing seemed forced, and every time he looked at her, he quickly looked away. She studied him closely. She'd bet anything he hadn't come to see Drew about fixing his car's muffler. It was something else that had brought him here.

"Oh, no." She cradled her forehead in her hand. "Did you get in trouble?"

He glanced at her. "No. Why would you ask that?"

"I just think something huge brought you to Deadhorse, and your excuse of bringing your car for Drew to look at is lame. It'd take more than that to make me come here." She shrugged. "Something's up, and you can tell me. I won't tell a soul."

"You'll have to wait. I want to tell you when Drew's here." He opened the microwave and removed the defrosted meat. "Besides, I don't want to talk about what brought me here yet when I haven't heard about all the exciting things you've been doing."

"Cruel, Satchel, cruel. My life would kill a man like you." She pushed the broiler pan across the counter. Then she realized whatever he had to share with them must be bothering him more than he was saying, because he'd made the long trip from Seattle to Eastern Oregon.

Three months of bad news was more than a single person should have to put up with, and she'd reached her quota. She watched, fascinated, as Gary stripped the potatoes of their peels. Whatever had happened, she could help. She only had to convince him to let her tag along when he went back home.

Also check out these titles from Debra Kayn:

Wildly

Seductively

Conveniently

Breathing His Air

In the mood for more Crimson Romance?
Check out *Wynter's Journey* by Jennifer DeCuir at
CrimsonRomance.com.